Mama and the Alien Warrior

TREASURED BY THE ALIEN

Honey Phillips

Bex McLynn

Disclaimer
*This book is a work of fiction. Names, characters, places,
and incidents are products of the author's imagination or are used
fictitiously and are not to be construed as real. Any resemblance to
actual events, locales, organizations, or people, living or dead, is
entirely coincidental.*

Cover Design by Cameron Kamenicky and
Naomi Lucas
Edited by Lindsay York at LY Publishing Services

ISBN-13: 978-1096979173

Chapter One

"**F**ireworks, Mama!" The excited little voice finally penetrated Abby's sleep-fogged brain.

She cracked open an eye to see her daughter standing by the bed in her pink fuzzy jammies, her long blonde hair tangled around her face.

"What is it, baby?"

"There's fireworks! I sawed a big flash of light outside my window."

Abby opened her other eye and squinted at her clock. Three o'clock in the morning? Running a maternity home meant that it wasn't the first time she'd been awakened at this hour, but it was usually due to one of her girls going into labor.

She peered out the window but could see only darkness. "I think you must have dreamed it, Lucie."

"I didn't, Mama. Honest."

"Okay, sweetie," she said yawning, then lifted the covers. "Why don't you crawl in here with me then and we'll wait to see if the fireworks come back?"

Lucie didn't hesitate. She dove under the covers, snuggling against Abby when she drew her close. Abby loved having the warm little body tucked against hers. She buried her nose in her daughter's silky hair, catching the scent of baby shampoo and bubblegum. Lucie had been sleeping in her big girl bed for over a year now, but Abby had to admit that her own bed felt less lonely with her daughter at her side. Especially since she hadn't shared it with anyone in the past, what was it—more than three years now? Three and a half years since she'd adopted her niece, and three years since John had walked out on her, unable to handle a child interrupting his lifestyle.

Abby didn't regret her decision in the slightest, especially now with her daughter safe in her arms, not left alone by a drug-addled mother.

She dropped a kiss on Lucie's head. "Go back to sleep, baby."

Abby's own eyes were just closing when a blinding flash lit up the room.

"See, Mama, I tolds you!"

That flash had not resembled fireworks in the least. What's more, it had seemed to come from inside the house. Was one of the girls playing some kind of game?

"Stay here, Lucie," she ordered as she climbed out of bed.

The air was cool enough that she pulled an old sweater over her sleep pants and tank as she headed for the door. Her bedroom and Lucie's room were at the back of the rambling old house, behind the shared kitchen, dining, and living areas. The girls' bedrooms were all on the second floor and she headed for the grand staircase that led upstairs. When she reached the big archway leading from the dining room to the entrance hall, shock held her motionless as she tried to understand what she was seeing.

Two strange men dressed in severe black suits stood at the bottom of the stairs, two more at the top. Amber, her newest resident, floated between them, her eyes closed and her long dark hair dangling as her body drifted down the stairs. As soon as she reached the bottom, one of the men pressed an instrument to her wrist and stepped back. The faintest burning smell reached Abby just as another flash of light filled her vision. As soon as she recovered from the searing impact to her retinas, she realized Amber was gone. That realization finally broke through her paralyzed shock and she stepped into the hallway.

"Who are you? What the hell are you doing?"

At her words, the men turned towards her and she was suddenly completely certain that they were not men. Their skin was white, not merely pale like human skin, but rather the smooth, flawless white of plastic. Matte black hair could perhaps have passed, but their eyes glowed with an unnatural red light and their features were just a little too long and angular to read as normal. This close, she could see that what she had taken for a suit was actually a uniform of some kind.

"Who are you?" she repeated, her voice shaking.

One of the men said something in a language she was quite sure didn't exist anywhere on Earth, and the other stepped towards her. She tried to back away, but he grabbed her with an abnormally fast movement, his grip cold and unbreakable. With his other hand, he lifted a syringe and jabbed it into her arm. The burning pain scorched through her, followed by an overwhelming dizziness as her vision started to fade. Just as she began to pass out, she heard Lucie's voice.

"Mama!"

Desperate to protect her daughter, she tried to struggle but her limbs wouldn't respond.

"Don't... don't hurt..."

The room spun and the world went black.

"Mama. Mama, please wake up." Lucie's voice came from a long way away as she drifted in a cold, dark world.

"Mama, I's scared."

Lucie's fearful voice finally penetrated, and she

forced her way back to consciousness. Her eyes watered when she tried to open them, halfway blinded by a bright, white light. She squinted against the glare, searching for her daughter's face. Lucie hovered over her and burst into tears when Abby opened her eyes.

"Ssh, baby. It's going to be all right." She pulled her daughter against her, Lucie's small body reassuringly warm and solid in her arms. Humming to her daughter despite the throbbing ache in her head, she tried to rock Lucie but her body felt heavy and lethargic. As the fog from whatever she'd been given began to clear, she noticed a burning sensation on her right wrist. Forcing her eyes to focus, she saw a long string of symbols etched onto her arm.

"Me too, Mama." Lucie's lip trembled as she held out her wrist next to Abby's. "It hurts."

The sight of the obscene mark on her daughter's delicate skin sent a flood of icy rage sweeping through her, clearing the last remnants of confusion from her head. Those bastards in the black suits were going to pay for this. Still holding Lucie close, she sat up and took in her surroundings.

They were in a sterile white room with glass walls on two sides and dull white metal walls on the other two. Four beds lined each side of the room and her girls, all of them still unconscious, occupied five of them. One wall overlooked a wide corridor, and the other side was lined with two sets of cabinets separated by a counter arrayed with an alarming variety of strange-looking instruments. Through the other glass wall, she could see a second white room, this one filled with clear plastic cribs. At least half of the cribs were occupied, and she thought she could identify the three babies belonging to her girls. There were two more human babies and one tiny green one who was obviously not human. The setup reminded her of a hospital—or a lab—and the strong antiseptic smell that permeated the air only reinforced that impression.

"Where are we, Mama?"

"I don't know." Her mind was still wrestling with the idea that the men who had come to the house had not been men after all. And if they weren't men, where was she now? "Did you see anybody before I woke up?"

"Just those mean men."

"Mean men?"

"The ones in black." Her lip trembled again. "I don't like them."

"I don't either, baby. Let's check on the girls, okay?"

"Okay." A tiny smile peeped out for the first time. "Elaina makes a lot of noise when she sleeps."

"But we don't have to tell her that," Abby said gently.

Keeping Lucie's hand firmly tucked in hers, she checked on the girls. All of them were still sleeping, although Cassie and TeShawna were starting to stir. Molly and Amber worried her the most. The other girls had recently had their babies, but these two were still pregnant. What effect would the sleeping potion in that syringe have on their unborn babies?

Returning to her cot, she lifted her daughter onto her lap. "Do you remember what happened, Lucie?"

Lucie hung her head. "I didn't want to wait so's I followed you. The mean man grabbed you and you fell down. Then he grabbed me." She looked up, tears welling in her big brown eyes. "He had a needle. I don't like needles. And I didn't even get a sticker."

"I don't think they're anywhere near as nice as Dr. Becky." Lucie's pediatrician always rewarded Lucie after she had her shots.

"They look funny. Who are they, Mama?"

"I don't know, baby," she said again, wishing she had some answers.

"What do they want?"

"I wish I knew."

Chapter Two

A little while later, the girls began to wake up. Cassie took the news that they appeared to have been taken by aliens with grim acceptance. She had already been through so much in her short life that she had cultivated a cynical shell that was rarely breached, although Abby could see her hands shaking. The other girls dissolved into tears as Abby did her best to comfort them. Molly, her fragile little sixteen-year-old, cried silently, big tears rolling down her cheeks.

"Aliens, Miss Abby?" TeShawna finally asked, wiping angrily at her cheeks. "Really?" A street smart girl with a defiant attitude, she was one of the first to recover.

"I know it sounds crazy, but they didn't look human." Abby gestured at the room. "And does this look like anywhere you've ever been?"

"Lotta places I ain't been," she muttered, then sighed. "But yeah, ain't never seen nothing like this before."

"What about our babies?" Elaina went to the glass wall that looked into the next room. The babies were also beginning to stir, and Cassie and TeShawna joined her at the wall.

"Mikie's gonna be gettin' hungry soon." Elaina crossed her arms over her breasts.

As if in response to her words, Mikie woke up. They couldn't hear him, but they could all see him as his mouth opened and his face started to turn red. All of the babies were completely naked, lying on plain white pads, with a glass dome covering each crib. The domes were apparently not soundproof because the other babies began to respond to Mikie's crying, and soon all of them were crying except the little green baby. Elaina started to sob, and even Cassie sniffled as they helplessly watched their crying children.

Narrow tubes suddenly emerged from the ceiling, one above each crib, and snaked down through an opening that appeared in the top of each dome. Each tube had a tip that resembled a nipple, and the nipple was aimed at each wailing mouth. The attempt was not successful. Three of the babies clamped down on the nipple eagerly, then immediately spat it back out again. The other two wouldn't even attempt it, while the little green baby just lay there silently.

A few agonizing minutes passed. All of the girls were crying again now and Abby fought back her own tears. Lucie clung to her leg, her lip starting to tremble. Dammit! There had to be some way to get the girls and their babies back together. She looked around desperately, wondering if she could break through the wall, but the cots were fastened to the floor.

While she tried to think of a solution, several of the aliens appeared in the corridor. Looking at them now under the bright lights, she wondered how she could ever have mistaken them for human. Everything about them was just slightly wrong enough to make the hairs on the back of her neck rise. And yet the differences could have been attractive if it hadn't been for the utter disdain with which their strange red eyes surveyed the women.

Lucie tightened her grip on Abby's leg but her little chin lifted. The other girls gathered behind Abby, the sight of the aliens stunning them into silence. Cassie straightened, dashing her tears away, but Molly whimpered under her breath.

"Damn, you wasn't lying. They're aliens all right," TeShawna muttered. She, too, straightened, her body poised for battle. "What do they want?"

"I don't know." Abby took a quick look at the terrified girls, all of them her responsibility. Her heart pounded but she assumed the firm, confident expression that had carried her through so many negotiations back in her corporate days. "But I'm going to try and find out." She gently unfolded Lucie's fingers. "You stay here with Cassie, okay?"

"Don't leave me!"

"I'm not going to leave you. I'll be right there where you can see me." She hoped.

"Come on, little bit. You stay here and help me be brave," Cassie said. Lucie hesitated, then nodded and dove against Cassie. The older girl hugged her and nodded to Abby. "Go see what those bast—what those men want."

Praying that her face appeared calm, Abby clenched her fists and approached the corridor wall. Two aliens moved around examining data readings while another alien, obviously the leader, questioned one of his subordinates. From the questioned man's hunched posture, it didn't appear to be a positive conversation. Nothing that they said was audible to her, but she hoped they had listening devices.

"Excuse me," she said firmly. The leader glanced at her with those disdainful red eyes and just as quickly dismissed her. The subordinate also glanced in her direction, then started talking very rapidly.

"Look, I don't know what you want with us, but those babies need their mothers. Now."

The subordinate kept talking, going as far as to touch the leader's sleeve before hastily withdrawing his fingers. She had a moment to notice that they had six digits before a section of the wall in front of her opened.

Looming over her, the leader addressed her

impatiently. His tone sounded demanding, but she didn't understand the rapid clicks that made up his language.

She kept her gaze locked on him. "I don't understand you."

The leader and his assistant conferred, then the subordinate beckoned her forward. With a hesitant glance at Lucie, still wrapped in Cassie's arms, she stepped out into the corridor.

The man pointed to his mouth and then his ear, repeating the gestures after pointing at her.

"I don't understand. What do you want?"

He shook his head and made the movements again.

"You... want to give me something to make me understand?"

He nodded.

"Very well." Her courage almost failed when he pulled out another syringe, but she looked at Lucie and was able to stand her ground.

Someone had to be able to communicate with these monsters.

The assistant approached, keeping his movement slow and deliberate, and swiped behind her ear with a cool fluid. She could only hope that sanitizing the area was a positive sign. His hand clamped down on her shoulder and before she could react, he inserted the needle. A bolt of fiery agony erupted in her head. Her mouth opened but no sound emerged, her system too shocked to scream. If it hadn't been for the firm grip on her shoulder, she would have collapsed. Fortunately, the pain passed quickly, leaving her weak and shaking but she forced herself to straighten. As soon as he felt her move, the alien removed his hand.

"Do you understand me now?" the leader demanded.

"Yes. What are—?"

"It is not your place to ask questions. The product is not accepting nourishment. What needs to be done?"

"The product?" Her mouth dropped open. "Do you mean the babies?"

He waved an eerie six-fingered hand. "The name does not matter. Why are they not accepting nourishment?"

"I don't know about the others, but the three you took from my house are still being fed by their mothers."

"The breeders must feed them?"

Her eyes narrowed. "Their *mothers* must feed them."

After another conference with his subordinate, too fast and quiet for her to follow, he nodded. "Very well. They may have access for the feeding period." He turned to one of the men still working at the counter. "Transfer the incubators."

A gap opened between the two rooms and three of the cribs floated through. The girls immediately went to their children, although Cassie paused long enough to pass Lucie over to Amber. The gap began to close, leaving two squalling infants and the silent alien child.

Abby pointed into the other room. "Wait a minute. What about the other babies?"

He made a gesture that was too minimal to be called a shrug. "Some product loss is inevitable."

It took every ounce of self-control she had not to smack his arrogant face. Instead, she forced an even tone and prayed the girls would understand. "Why don't you let me see if we can nourish the others as well?"

The leader considered, then inclined his head. "Very well."

He gestured to one of this men, and the cribs containing the other two human children began to move.

11

Abby looked at the tiny, silent alien baby and her heart ached. "What about that one?"

The subordinate cast a nervous glance at the leader, then said quickly, "Human nourishment would not be appropriate for a Cire infant. The product is very weak."

"A foolish investment—and the purchase will be coming from your share," the leader said coldly to the other man. "It was not worth the additional outlay."

Abby bit her lip. She looked at the tiny baby again and knew she had to at least try and save it. "Do you have a bottle?" When the subordinate looked puzzled, she added. "A small container with a nipple? For hand-feeding?"

"How primitive," the leader said, already starting to turn away.

"If she—if the product lived, it would be valuable, Commander Khaen," the other man said quickly. "It would be a simple matter to create this *bottle*."

"Very well. You may make the attempt," Khaen said, as if he were granting a great favor. Then he turned and walked away.

Wishing she had something to throw after him, she turned back to the other man. "You can make a bottle?"

"Yes." He hurried over to the counter and began pulling out pieces of equipment. She noticed that the two other aliens working there sneered at him, mirroring the same contempt as the leader; however, he was back in a few minutes with a serviceable bottle filled with a rather disgusting grey fluid.

"It's nutritionally complete," he assured her when he saw her eyeing the liquid dubiously. He manipulated a touchscreen and the alien baby's crib began to move into the girls' room.

"Thank you. What's your name?"

"Me?" He looked shocked that she asked. "I am Kwaret." Behind him, the two others made a clearly derogatory noise. He flinched but didn't respond.

"Thank you, Kwaret. I don't know if it's going to work, but I have to try."

Mama and the Alien Warrior

Chapter Three

A s soon as she stepped back into the room and the panel closed behind her, Lucie came rushing over. Abby gave her a quick hug and lifted her up onto her hip. Molly and Amber rocked the two strange babies, both still whimpering, their cries tugging at Abby's heart.

"What are we going to do, Miss Abby?" Amber looked stricken. "They're hungry."

"About that..." She studied the other three girls. Mikie was already half-asleep at Elaina's breast and TeShawna held Vanessa up on her shoulder. Cassie still nursed Angel. "Have you girls ever heard of wet nurses?"

"What's that?" Amber asked.

"They're women who will nurse another woman's child if that woman isn't capable of feeding her baby herself."

TeShawna, of course, caught on first and her eyes narrowed. "You wanting me to feed one of them strange babies?"

"Yes. I know it's a lot to ask, but if we can't find a way to feed them, they'll die," she said gently. "You saw what happened when the aliens tried."

"Die?" Lucie asked, her eyes big. "You can't let the babies die."

"Don't worry, Lucie girl," Elaina said quickly. "We'll feed them."

"Speak for yourself," Cassie said bitterly. "I don't even have enough milk for one."

Abby shot her a worried look. It was true that Cassie was having difficulty nursing. They had been preparing to put Angel on formula because the baby hadn't been gaining weight.

"I'll do it," TeShawna said. "But Vanessa goes first."

"Thank you, girls."

Mikie gave a loud burp, as if in agreement, and they all laughed. There was a slightly hysterical edge to it, but Abby would rather have the laughter than have the girls worrying about their situation. She really didn't want to explain to them that the aliens had referred to them as breeders.

"Don't they have any diapers around this place?" Elaina asked. "Mikie usually has a big poop after he eats."

"I'll ask." Abby returned to the front wall, Lucie still on her hip. Kwaret was nowhere in sight but the other two aliens were still there.

"Excuse me."

Just like before, they ignored her.

"We need diapers for the children."

Still no response.

"Look, if we don't get some type of um, sanitary supplies, it's going to get awfully messy in here."

One of them finally turned to her, touching a button so that his voice sounded inside the room.

"We no longer use your primitive methods," he sneered. "The incubators are equipped to handle bodily waste."

Knowing that Lucie watched everything with wide eyes, Abby bit back her retort and forced out a thank you.

"Mama, I gotta pee too." Lucie's urgent whisper reminded her that the babies weren't the only ones in need of sanitary arrangements.

With a muffled sigh, she addressed the aliens again. "What about us? You don't expect us to use the incubators as well, do you?"

The alien had started to turn away but he stopped at her words. A condescending smile spread across his stark white face and she wondered if he would actually tell her that exact thing, but after a brief pause, he gestured at the rear of their room.

"Standard facilities are provided. Any civilized being would recognize that."

He turned his back on her and she bit her tongue once more.

"What'd he say, Mama?" Lucie squirmed anxiously in her arms.

"He said it's back there. Let's go see if we can find it."

Fortunately, they discovered that one of the panels opened to reveal a small bathroom. The facilities were oddly shaped but similar enough to an Earth bathroom to be self-explanatory. Lucie giggled when the toilet first washed her, then dried her with a blast of warm air.

Their immediate needs resolved, they returned to the main room. TeShawna and Elaina now nursed the two new babies while Cassie rocked Angel.

"The alien said the cribs would work like diapers," she told them.

Molly made a face. "Vanessa already peed on me."

"That's my girl," TeShawna said with a grin.

"Well, I don't want to be pooped on," Amber said firmly and laid Mikie in one of the cribs. He almost immediately fulfilled his mother's prophecy and they all watched in fascination as the pad absorbed the results and followed it with a fine mist and a spray of warm air.

"Yucky!" Lucie said, her face scrunched up.

"Are you kidding?" Amber picked up Mikie and examined his spotless bottom. "That's magic, baby girl."

While the girls admired the cribs, Abby turned to the little alien baby, still lying silently, her eyes wide open. Very carefully, she picked up the tiny figure, her throat tightening at the slight weight as she cradled her. For the first time, the baby made a tiny noise and seemed to snuggle closer.

"Who's that, Mama?" Lucie peered over her shoulder.

"It's another baby."

"I ain't putting no green baby to my boobs," TeShawna said loudly. Then she took a second look at the tiny figure and sighed. "She's awful skinny though. Hell, I reckon I can. I let Nick at 'em and he was a worthless prick." Nick was Vanessa's father and had abandoned TeShawna two months before she gave birth.

"What's a prick?" Lucie piped up.

"Something I hope you never have to worry about," TeShawna said, with an apologetic glance at Abby.

"Thank you for offering, TeShawna, but the aliens said human milk wouldn't work. They gave me that." Abby gave the bottle a dubious look. "Let's see if she'll take it. Hand me the bottle, baby."

Lucie picked it up and made a face. "It's cold."

"If that's a bathroom back there, I can run it under some warm water. Maybe heat it up some?" Amber offered.

"That would be great. Thanks, Amber."

Abby looked down at the baby to see she was looking back up at her. The tiny figure looked so helpless with her little sticklike limbs naked and exposed. The room was a comfortable temperature, but she worried about the child catching a chill. "Lexi, help me get this sweater off, please."

By the time she wrestled her sweater off and wrapped it around the infant, Amber had returned. When

Abby put the bottle to the baby's lips, her mouth remained closed. Abby cuddled her closer, then stroked her finger along the tiny mouth until it opened a fraction. She managed to get a drop of the warm liquid on the baby's tongue, and after a startled pause, her mouth opened and she began sucking with frantic urgency. Relief flooded Abby's body.

"What's the baby's name?" Lucie had been standing at her elbow the whole time, watching curiously.

"I don't know. We'll have to give her one. What do you think would be a good name?"

"Oscar," Lucie said immediately. "Like on Sesame Street."

Abby hid a smile as she looked down at the baby. It was true that she had big dark eyes, a wide mouth, and an almost non-existent nose, but her smooth green skin was a long way from the Muppet's wild fur.

"Oscar is a boy's name, sweetie. What about Lily?"

Lucie frowned at the baby. "What about Tiana? She was green when she was a frog."

Abby looked down at the tiny alien face, so strange but somehow still so sweet, and nodded. "I think that's perfect, baby."

Tiana was still sucking hungrily but her eyes remained on Abby's face. She felt a small flutter and looked down to see a tiny green band clinging to her wrist.

"Look, Mama! She gots a tail."

"So she does."

"What's it for?"

"I don't know that it's for anything." But even as she spoke, the tiny tail pulsed around her wrist. It reminded her of the way Lucie had kneaded her breast while she gave her a bottle and her heart tugged. *I'll take care of you, little one,* she promised silently.

A short time later, one of the aliens spoke to her through the wall. "Return the product to the incubators."

"What do you mean?" Most of the babies had fallen asleep in their mother's—or their surrogate mother's—arms. Tiana was snuggled against Abby, her big eyes finally closed. Lucie, tucked against her other side, slept with her head on Abby's knee.

"You have provided nourishment. Return it to the incubators."

"Why can't they stay with their mothers?" She tried to keep her voice calm, seeing that the girls were starting to look alarmed.

"The breeders provide nourishment only. The product no longer belongs to them. It would be as well if they accept this now."

"But they will need more nourishment," she protested.

"They will be returned at the appropriate time." When she didn't respond, his face grew even colder. "If you do not comply, you will be punished and the product will be taken anyway."

"I understand." *You asshole.* Taking a deep breath, she turned to the girls. "We have to put the babies back in the cribs. I think they're going to return them to the other room."

"But why?" Elaina wailed, holding Mikie tighter.

"They, uh, think it's better for them. But they'll bring them back to be fed again."

"Like we're some kind of goddamn cows?" TeShawna muttered. Abby was afraid she was only too right.

"I'm sorry, girls, but I think they're going to do it anyway." She gestured at the wall where the alien had his hand raised to open the panel. With some more muttered cursing, and not a few tears, the girls obeyed. Her own heart ached when she had to lay Tiana back in her crib. The little face crumpled but she remained as silent as before, never taking her eyes off of Abby. They all watched helplessly as the cribs moved back into the other room and the wall between them closed.

Mama and the Alien Warrior

Chapter Four

"**S**ir!" Hrebec Nak'Charen, Captain of the Confederated Planets patrol cutter *Defiance*, closed his eyes at the sound of the eager young voice outside his quarters.

He had a great fondness for the young officer, indeed somewhat more of a liking than was quite fair; however, he found himself in no mood to deal with Ensign Ribel's latest enthusiasm. But he held the reins of command in his weary hands and it was his duty to be available to his men.

"Come."

Ribel burst in with more haste than dignity, his tail whipping wildly. "Sir, we have detected a Vedeckian slave ship at the edge of the quadrant."

"And?"

Ribel tilted his head with a confused look. "I assumed you would want to mount a rescue mission?"

Hrebec contemplated his hands. It was, of course, the right thing to do. The Vedeckians were a disgrace to the Confederated Planets. They masqueraded as merchants but their main business involved the illegal sale of living beings —and unfortunately, these days the Vedeckians had all too many buyers. However, he suspected that Ribel's excitement derived from another source rather than the desire to investigate a possible violation of the law.

"And what do you think will be the result of the mission?" he asked.

"We will free their slaves, of course." Hrebec's skeptical silence had the desired result, and Ribel flushed and continued. "And perhaps they will have females fit for mating."

As he suspected. Hrebec sighed and contemplated his junior. Ribel was so young. His lamella had barely started to form. Only a single ridge adorned his head and his chest remained as smooth as a babe's. He was one of the few who had survived the artificial wombs that had been their people's last desperate attempt to salvage their race.

"Ensign Ribel, do you remember what happened the last time?"

Ribel's flush deepened, his normal emerald complexion turning almost black with embarrassment. The *Defiance* had rescued a cargo of Villae females. Ribel had been convinced that the adorable, dainty little creatures would prove to be ideal mates. Unfortunately, he had found through personal contact that they were, in fact, entirely incompatible with Cire anatomy. That unfortunate experience did not seem to have deterred his enthusiasm.

Hrebec had long ago accepted that the Cires were a dying race. Their time had come, and no matter how much he wished he could have saved his people, no matter the price he had paid for those attempts, they wouldn't escape their fate.

"It is part of our job to make sure that they are not transporting illegal passengers. We will investigate." He held up a hand when Ribel looked up eagerly. "However, this is a rescue mission only. If it turns out that there are illegal females on board, they will be returned to their original destination. This is not a mating opportunity. Do you understand me?"

"Yes, sir," Ribel responded, but Hrebec could tell that his excitement hadn't dimmed. He shook his head.

"Wait until we are within firing range. Then hail them and tell them to prepare for inspection."

"Yes, sir."

"I will join you on the bridge shortly."

Once the door closed behind the young officer, Hrebec sighed. He wished he still felt even a spark of the same enthusiasm, the same hopefulness, that Ribel did, but Ribel was too young. He hadn't lived through the millions of deaths, through the hopeless attempts to reproduce by artificial technology, through the agony of knowing that your race would die out.

But Hrebec had a job to do and his job did include stopping the illegal transportation of slaves. And even though he knew there was no chance that there would be breeding females, his tail stirred at the thought. Sternly suppressing the unruly appendage, he headed for the bridge.

In the dim light of the rest period, Abby stared up at the ceiling and rubbed her wrist thoughtfully as she worried about her girls. The burn mark had healed during the time they'd been on the ship. As best she could tell, it had been two weeks since they were taken, and she knew no more about their destination now than she did on her first morning. As she grimly considered the possibilities, Lucie shoved her elbow into her side and she winced. Her daughter had slept with her every night since they had been taken, and while she loved having her close, she was a restless sleeper and Abby's nights were not peaceful.

The days had settled into a monotonous routine. The aliens still insisted on separating the babies once the girls fed them, although they brought them back on a regular schedule. When Kwaret was on duty, he allowed them a longer period with the infants, but even he eventually insisted that they return them to their cribs. It never got any easier to watch them be silently carried away and her heart ached every time she considered that one day soon, it would be a permanent separation.

She dreaded the day they would take Tiana as much as if she were truly her mother. The little girl had rapidly wound her way into her heart.

Other than worrying about the future, keeping Lucie busy became Abby's biggest challenge. Although the girls all tried to keep her occupied, an energetic four-year-old wasn't suited to one-room living. To Abby's surprise, Kwaret also helped. He provided Abby with a few markers and some paper, along with a small globe of some type of rubbery substance which served as an adequate ball. So far, they'd managed to keep the small toys hidden from Commander Khaen.

The leader had returned on the second day demanding proof that the babies had been eating. He then ordered Elaina to feed the red-headed baby, now named Ginger, before she fed Mikie. Of course, Abby had protested, but he only gave her a cold stare.

"The female product is more valuable. If the breeder does not comply, I will eliminate the male product."

Appalled by the commander's threat, Abby had had no choice but to urge Elaina to comply.

At least Elaina had plenty of milk and didn't struggle like Cassie. TeShawna was feeding the other new baby, now called Lily, as well as her own Vanessa, but after three days of watching Cassie trying to feed Angel, TeShawna went and stood over Cassie. "Hand her here."

"No, she's mine." Cassie glared at the bigger girl.

"Not if she starves," TeShawna said coldly before her face softened. "Girl, she's still gonna be your baby. I'm feeding half the world anyway. Might as well add her to the list."

Cassie relented and Abby had breathed a silent prayer of relief. Now all of the babies were thriving, even Tiana, who kicked her arms and legs happily whenever she saw Abby coming.

Abby continued to worry about Molly. The young girl seemed to get thinner and more distant every day, retreating into herself. Unlike Amber, who frequently put her hand on her stomach or talked about baby names, Molly seemed as removed from her impending child as she was from the rest of the girls.

By her calculations, both girls had less than a week to go. When she had asked Kwaret if the ship was equipped for childbirth, he had stuttered nervously in a way that did not give her confidence. She found herself torn between hoping they would arrive at their destination, which presumably would have more sophisticated medical facilities, and fearing what that destination would bring.

Their fate was another subject that made Kwaret stutter. The one piece of information she had dragged out of him was that because the girls had already proven themselves to be breeders, they would be of great value and well treated. But where did that leave her? She'd never had a child and her age made it less likely that she ever would. But if she needed to sell herself as a breeder in order to keep Lucie safe, that's what she would do. As she grimly considered her possible fate, an alarm sounded.

Red lights began flashing in the corridor, along with the piercing shriek of the alarm. Lucie started to cry as the girls sat up, confused and frightened. Abby put her arms around Lucie and rocked her soothingly but her eyes went to the next room. The babies had been awoken as well, Mikie already red-faced and obviously squalling even though they couldn't hear him. Although Tiana wasn't crying, her eyes were open and scared.

"What's happening, Mama?" Lucie sniffled as she started to recover from the shock of being woken so unexpectedly.

"I don't know, baby."

The girls started to gather around her. Even Molly roused herself from her usual apathy to join them as they waited in tense silence. The alarm cut off, and the sudden silence became as deafening as the noise had been. The red lights continued to flash as strange men strode into the corridor. Not men, Abby realized, more aliens. Massive, heavily muscled aliens with reptilian features, ridged hairless skulls, and an intimidating array of weapons. She couldn't help but wonder if they hadn't fallen from the frying pan into the fire.

Chapter Five

Hrebec stepped into the third transportation bay, already braced for what he would find. The first bay had been packed with majinda plants, which were not illegal to transport but were illegal to sell on Karmad due to their effects on the natives, although he had no proof that was their intended destination. The second bay was filled with illegal furs and mounted specimens of rare species that were under planetary quarantine. Their presence alone would command a long jail sentence for the seven-person crew—now four, since three had foolishly refused to surrender.

As soon as he entered the small area, his appalled gaze went to the incubators. A horrible vision flashed before his eyes: row after row of the plastic domes, gradually growing cold and empty as their efforts failed and the children died. These were not Cire babies, but it didn't matter. He couldn't leave them to suffer.

"Get them out of there!" he roared. "Get them out now!"

Sedlit went to the control panel, quickly searching for the entrance controls. In the process, he activated the audio controls, enabling him to hear the infants crying, along with a second set of cries.

As Hrebec strode into the nursery, a distinct sentence halted him.

"Don't you dare touch them. They're our children."

His tail quivered at the sound of the low, furious voice, and despite his desire to free the infants, he found himself turning in that direction. A small figure stood on the other side of the glass. She was most definitely not Cire, but as his gaze traveled from a head of short tousled dark hair to big grey eyes and then down over a very curvy and indisputably female figure, he didn't find that a lack. His tail twitched and his shaft started to thicken before he forced it under control.

"Who are you?" he demanded.

"I'm Abigail Wentworth. We're humans, stolen from a planet called Earth, and those are our children. I'm not going to let you take them away."

Since she currently stood in a Vedeckian cell, there was no way for her to prevent him, but her fierceness impressed him. He also had no intention of separating children from their mothers.

"Sedlit, can you unlock the second room?"

"Just a minute, sir. I think it's… Yes, that's it."

The wall between the two rooms opened. He was vaguely aware of the other females gathering behind Abigail Wentworth, but his attention remained fixed on her. With the panel open, he caught a hint of a sultry sweetness that shot straight to his shaft. His tail curved around in front of his leg, trying to get closer to the female. Her pale eyes, sparkling in the dim light, flickered to the incubators. As she made a wary step in that direction, he noticed a small female clinging to her leg.

"You have a child?"

"Yes."

An unexpected feeling of disappointment rushed through him. She already had a mate. Stepping back slightly, he gestured for her to proceed. Keeping a wary eye on him, she stepped into the room and gestured for the other females to proceed to the incubators. One hand on her daughter, she followed them, then picked up a… a Cire infant?

"You have one of our children?" he asked sharply.

"She's mine." Abigail cuddled the baby with one arm and pulled the older child close with the other.

"She?"

The room literally spun around him as he heard the gasps from his crew.

"Yes. Why does it matter?" Before he could respond, she raised her chin defiantly. "I know that you think female 'product' has more value, but I won't let you take her. She needs me."

"Did you give birth to her?" he demanded impatiently.

He had experience enough with other races to read the hesitation on her face, and he knew the answer even before she shook her head. Some of his elation died, but he was still overcome to find a female Cire, alive. The Red Death had taken all of their women, and of the few babies to come full term in the artificial wombs, none had been female. This child's mere existence was a miracle.

"Where did she come from?"

"I don't know," Abigail said reluctantly, before her chin lifted again. "But she's mine now."

"Lieutenant Jedan, examine the logs. See if you can find any indication of where she was found. I will want to interrogate the prisoners as well."

"Yes, sir."

Unable to help himself, he stepped forward to take a closer look. The baby in Abigail's arms was impossibly small, but he could detect no sign of ill health and her wide dark eyes were bright. He took a deep breath, and Abigail's enticing scent washed over him. He was suddenly conscious that his tail was reaching for her—for her or the child—and that his men eagerly watched them.

As he started to step back, the small child at her side spoke up. "Are you Leonardo?"

Abigail made a little choking noise. "No, sweetie. Leonardo is just a cartoon."

He didn't quite follow the conversation, but he realized that he had failed to introduce himself. "I am Captain Hrebec. I represent the Confederated Planets. We have impounded this ship and arrested the crew. I will escort you to my ship, the *Defiance*."

"And then what?" she asked suspiciously.

"Then we will make arrangements for your return," he said firmly.

Behind him, he heard a few disappointed noises from his crew, and was conscious of the same feeling deep within his chest, but he ignored them. Their job was to free the captives and he had to keep that in mind. This job was all he had left.

Abby stared up at the big alien standing so close to her, too close for her to ignore the extremely well-defined muscles revealed by his tight white uniform. Everything about him intimidated her, from his overall size to his unabashedly alien appearance. It was almost impossible to believe that he and Tiana were the same species, although they shared the same wide lipless mouth, flat nose, and large black eyes. The resemblance ended there. His jade skin was several shades darker than Tiana's pale green, but more than that, unlike the baby's smooth little head, he had a series of dark ridges arching back over his forehead. More curved down his neck and across the top of his massive shoulders. There was one additional resemblance, she realized, as his tail curled around from behind him and headed in her direction.

Lucie giggled. "Look, Mama. He gots a tail just like Tiana."

She reached out an inquisitive hand just as Captain Hrebec pulled it back, an appalled look on his face.

"You mustn't touch, Lucie," she said, even as she glared at him. It wasn't like her daughter was going to hurt his precious tail.

"The child did nothing wrong," he said quickly. "Children are naturally curious." He addressed Lucie directly. "Would you like to touch it?"

"She can't understand you. I'm the only one who was provided with a translator."

He looked appalled for a second time and immediately raised his hand to one of the group of aliens gathered behind him. "Mekoi, the females will need translation devices."

"No, they don't." She pulled Lucie closer. "There's no need to subject them to the pain when we're just going home anyway."

"Pain?"

"When you implant the device? It hurts like hell."

This time, his expression turned thunderous; his dark eyes flashed, and she swore that his shoulders tensed. "It should not have hurt you. I promise you that we will not cause pain to your females. But it would be easier if they were able to communicate."

Abby bit her lip. Part of her instinctively wanted to trust the big alien, even though she knew better than to drop her guard. It also occurred to her that it would be easier for the aliens to separate them if she wasn't the only one capable of communicating. But in the end, it wasn't her decision. She turned to the girls. They had all grouped themselves behind her, each one holding a baby. Even Molly had picked up Ginger, although her hold on the infant was less secure than Abby would have liked.

"Girls, the captain has offered to give all of you translators so you can understand what they're saying. He says it won't hurt, but I can't try it for you first since I already have one. Do you want one?"

Lucie piped up. "I wants one, Mama. I wanna know what Leonardo is saying."

"I'm not sure that's a good idea, baby." She shot a nervous glance over her shoulder at the big alien.

"Why don't you wish the child to understand?" he asked.

"I don't want her hurt."

"I would never hurt a child." His outrage seemed genuine, but what if he didn't understand how easily a human child could be hurt?

TeShawna shrugged and stepped forward. "I'll try it out. I managed to push out a nine-pound baby. I ain't worried about a little pinprick."

Abby wouldn't have called the blazing agony of the injection a pinprick, but if TeShawna volunteered, she wouldn't try and stop her.

"You are a brave female," Hrebec told TeShawna gravely, and Abby had the oddest sense of... surely it wasn't jealousy? "Mekoi is our chief medical officer. He will perform the procedure."

"Yeah." TeShawna rolled her eyes. "Like I understood any of that."

A second alien stepped forward. He wasn't as big as Hrebec, or as heavily marked, but he was still an imposing figure. TeShawna gulped but she hid it behind her usual bravado.

Turning to Cassie, she passed her daughter over. "Hold Vanessa," she murmured. "Don't let nothing happen to her."

"Never," Cassie said quietly.

Dropping a kiss on her daughter's forehead, TeShawna stepped forward. "Okay, big guy. Let's see if you're lying."

The medic stepped forward. TeShawna wasn't a small girl by any means, but the alien dwarfed her sturdy figure. Abby noticed that his tail lashed anxiously as it kept trying to reach for TeShawna.

"Why's that thing trying to touch me?" TeShawna demanded.

Abby looked at Hrebec.

"It's an... instinct," he said reluctantly. "It is trying to offer comfort."

"He says it's trying to comfort you."

"Oh yeah? Not sure why a tail would be comforting," TeShawna muttered. "Unless it's like biting down on a bullet or something, like in one of those old movies you like."

Before Abby could respond, TeShawna reached out and grabbed hold of the tail that was once again flickering in her direction. The medic groaned and there was a shocked silence from the other aliens. Abby suddenly suspected that there was a lot more to the tail business than Hrebec had revealed.

The medic took a step closer and held up a syringe. TeShawna's skin went ashy but she jutted out her lip defiantly and took a firmer grasp on the tail. The alien's eyes fluttered but he shook his head, brushed a cloth behind TeShawna's ear, and then pressed the syringe against it before stepping back.

"Are you going to do it or what?" she demanded.

"It's already done," he said.

"It is? Oh. Oh! I understood you. You were right, big guy. That didn't hurt at all."

In her excitement, TeShawna pumped the medic's tail up and down, and from the look on his face, Abby didn't think he shared her relief.

"I think you should let go of his tail, TeShawna," she said quietly.

"His tail?" The girl looked down, and a hint of color actually darkened her cheeks as she hastily released him. "Sorry, big guy."

"It was my honor," he said with a deep bow and stepped back, his tail still trying to reach for TeShawna.

TeShawna hesitated for just a second, then turned to the other girls. "Nothing to it. Who's next?"

Cassie looked grim, but she handed both babies to TeShawna. "I'll do it. Better to know what they're saying."

When she stepped forward, Abby noticed that the medic's tail stayed firmly behind his back. Even as she decided to keep her mouth shut, she felt a gentle brush against her hip and looked down to see Hrebec's tail lightly touching her. Before she could react, he'd snatched it away, the same appalled look on his face.

"Comfort, huh?" she said skeptically. He didn't respond but the jade color of his cheeks darkened to emerald.

Within a few minutes, all of the girls except Molly had received the translator. The medic's tail had never reappeared.

"Me, Mama. Me next." Lucie was practically dancing with impatience.

Abby bit her lip and turned to Hrebec. "You promise

it won't hurt her?"

"I vow on Granthar's Hammer," he said solemnly.

When Abby gave a reluctant agreement, he gestured to the medic. As he approached with the syringe, Lucie's excitement suddenly died.

"It's going to be an owwie, isn't it?"

"No, baby. The captain promised."

Big brown eyes looked up at Hrebec anxiously. "I wanna hold your tail."

"Lucie—"

"Of course," Hrebec interrupted, his tail already flicking in front of Lucie. She grabbed it with both hands before Abby could prevent her and cradled it to her chest. Despite her reservations, Hrebec's hard face only softened. Mekoi stepped behind Lucie while she was still exploring the tail and touched the syringe to her neck.

"Okay, I's ready," she said, lifting her chin.

"It's already done, little one," Hrebec said.

"It didn't hurt."

"I told you it would not. I would never lie to you."

Lucie frowned up at him for a second before a sunny smile bloomed on her face. "Okay." She patted his tail and released it.

Abby could only pray that her daughter's faith, and her own, was not misplaced.

Mama and the Alien Warrior

Chapter Six

As Abby stared at Hrebec, another alien stepped up beside him. He was tall and muscular like the rest of the newcomers, but he appeared almost slight next to the big captain. His head was nearly smooth, lacking the ridges that Hrebec had, and she decided he must be quite young.

"What about the smallest female?" he asked. "She has not received the translator."

All three of them turned to look at Molly, and Abby saw her face go white. She swayed, and Abby took a step forward, but the young alien darted past her, catching Molly and Ginger before they fell. Abby was right behind him, hurriedly passing Tiana to Cassie on the way.

Molly hadn't quite passed out but she was trembling in the young alien's arms.

"Let me take Ginger," Abby said, retrieving the baby from the young girl's shaking hands. Elaina immediately stepped up to take her, and when Abby turned back, Molly was clutching the alien's arms and his tail was wrapped around her wrist.

"Oh no you don't," Abby said. "You put that thing away right now."

He flushed, but when he went to release Molly, she only clung more tightly. Abby cast a helpless look up at Hrebec but he was frowning down at the couple as well.

"Perhaps she would feel safer with the translator?" the youngster said diffidently. "Can you ask her?"

Molly had looked up at him when he spoke, her eyes fastened on his mouth with an almost painful intensity. A sinking feeling filled Abby's stomach. Molly was constantly on the lookout for a protector. That was how she'd ended up pregnant at sixteen, the victim of a much older man who had promised to take care of her. Instead, he'd abandoned her on Abby's doorstep as soon as she had started to show.

"Molly, do you want the translator?"

"Is that what he asked?" Her voice was a thin whisper.

"Yes, but it's *your* decision."

"I'd like to be able to talk to him," she said shyly.

Abby had a sudden impulse to shake the girl and tell her to stop living in a fantasyland. Her salvation wasn't dependent on a man any more than Abby's had been. Instead, she bit back her feelings with a sigh. The translator was probably a good idea under the circumstances. The medic had joined them and she gave him a reluctant nod. While Molly clung to the young alien and his tail clung to her, Mekoi performed the injection.

"How will I know if it worked?" Molly asked.

"Can you understand me?" he asked.

"Oh yes," she breathed.

"I'm Ribel," he said solemnly. "What is your name?"

"I'm Molly."

"That's a beautiful name."

The two of them gazed into each other's eyes with too much intensity for Abby's liking. Hrebec's tail brushed against her hip again, and she gave it an impatient yank. When he turned a startled look in her direction, she jerked her head at the young couple. It was his crew. He needed to put a stop to all the lovey-dovey mush before it got out of hand.

"Ensign Ribel, it is time to return to the ship. Please ensure that the Vedeckians are prepared for transport."

"But, sir. I thought that—"

"Now, Ensign Ribel."

"Yes, sir." The despondent look on his face as he unwrapped his tail from around Molly's wrist made Abby wonder just how old he was. Molly watched him with a trembling lip as he gently let her go.

"I'll see you," he promised quickly. He shot a nervous glance at Hrebec before heading to the door.

Hrebec watched his young officer depart and cursed under his breath. So much for containing his enthusiasm. They hadn't even been on this accursed ship for half an hour and Ribel already displayed signs of mating fever. Although it was... interesting that Ribel's tail had become involved. That was usually reserved for a true mate. First Mekoi then Ribel had displayed signs of possessiveness. Even his own tail kept seeking out Abigail, and he couldn't help but remember the feel of her small, soft fingers on the sensitive skin. He looked down to find it heading for her again, but he forced it under control.

"Are you ready to depart?" he asked.

"Not like we got anything to carry, boss," one of the girls said. TeShawna, that was her name. A tall, sturdy girl with warm brown skin and a short cap of tight dark curls, she was obviously the most outspoken. And yet she directed an unexpectedly shy glance at Mekoi, who was watching her discreetly. Hrebec shook his head. Mekoi had worked with him in the doomed labs. He had never thought the quiet medic would be any more capable of moving past that experience than he was.

"I's tired, Mama." The young child yawned and leaned against Abigail, who once again cradled the Cire infant.

"Just a little longer, sweetie. Then we can go back to

bed." She turned to him, and he felt an unexpected pulse in his loins as their eyes met. "Do you have room for all of us?"

The ship was somewhat understaffed; a full complement hadn't chosen to accompany him on his self-imposed exile. If the men doubled up, there should be room. He would give Abigail and her children his rooms since they were the largest. He chose to ignore the fact that the thought of her in his quarters was immensely satisfying.

"Yes. My men can share."

"Hmm. The girls might want to share as well." She cast a discreet glance at the young girl who fascinated Ribel, and he understood her concern.

"That may be for the best," he agreed.

"And unless you want to take the cribs with us, we'll need supplies for the babies—diapers if nothing else."

"Diapers?"

Her cheeks turned a rather fascinating shade of pink, but she spoke evenly. "To cover their bottoms. For when they, um, urinate."

"Oh, of course." The ship was not supplied with anything of the kind. "Mekoi?"

"We have absorbent bandages. Those should work." Mekoi hesitated. "The temperature on the *Defiance* is cooler. The infants should be covered. The mothers as well." Hrebec saw him take a discreet glance at TeShawna's long, bare legs and he realized that all of the females were scantily attired. With the exception of Abigail, he thought with a twinge of regret. Long pants covered her legs and her upper body was swathed in some type of furry substance. The small female was also covered in fuzzy pink. But the Cire infant was unprotected.

He paused, then stripped off his uniform top and handed it to Abigail. "Wrap her in this."

Her eyes widened as she took in his bare chest and she licked her lips. The sight of her small pink tongue caused an immediate reaction in his cock, which he sternly ignored.

"Um, okay." She took the white shirt dubiously. "She might get it messy."

"That is not an issue."

A slight movement caught his eye. He turned his head and bit back a groan. Every one of his crew members had also stripped off their uniform tops. Mekoi was already approaching TeShawna. "Please accept this. For your child."

The look she gave him was halfway between suspicion and shyness, but she eventually nodded and took the garment. "I don't want her getting cold."

Each of his men approached the females and the infants were quickly swaddled. Only the smallest, Molly, refused a shirt, but she wasn't carrying a child.

Jedan assisted one of the other females who was carrying two babies. He hovered, his tail twitching. "Would you permit me to carry one of the infants? I do not wish you to be burdened."

This female had pale skin covered with speckles and it flushed pink at the request. She bit her lip and looked at Abigail.

"Promise me that he won't hurt the baby and he'll return her as soon as we get to your ship?" Abigail demanded quietly.

"I promise."

"It's okay, Elaina," she told the girl. "Just show him how to support her head." With a little fumbling, the move was accomplished, but he could see Jedan's tail already curling around the infant. The situation was rapidly getting out of control. He needed to get these distracting females back to the *Defiance* and safely stowed away.

"Mama, I's tired." The small voice drew his attention to the young child, now leaning heavily against Abigail's legs.

"I know, baby. Not much longer."

"Carry me."

Abigail looked at the Cire infant, then at her daughter. Before she could speak, he intervened.

"Would you permit me to carry you, little one? With your mother's permission, of course."

Abigail glared at him, but he knew she wouldn't refuse permission. How could she, when she had just told one of the young females that it was acceptable? Instead, she turned to her daughter. "Do you want Hrebec to carry you, Lucie?"

The child looked up at him gravely, then raised her arms in a trusting gesture that caused an unexpected ache in his chest. He reached down and carefully picked her up, her slight body almost unbelievably fragile.

"You's all bumpy," she said, running a curious finger across his lamella.

"Yes, I am," he agreed.

She tucked her head into his neck and closed her eyes. Her golden hair, soft and fragrant, brushed along his jaw. He tore his eyes away from her small figure and found Abigail watching him, an unreadable expression on his face.

"Let us depart," he said before turning to lead the way.

Chapter Seven

Abby hurried to follow Hrebec, determined not to let him out of her sight for a second. Despite her overall lack of faith in the male gender, she found herself inexplicably trusting the big alien. That did not mean, however, that she'd let him get more than an inch away from her while he carried Lucie. The sight of her daughter's small blonde head, snuggled into that massive green chest, tugged at her heart. She had no problems raising Lucie as a single mother, but she couldn't help wondering sometimes if her daughter was missing out.

Lucie hadn't started asking questions about her daddy yet, but Abby knew it was only a matter of time. Since her father was a worthless drug dealer, currently serving an extended prison sentence, she wasn't eager to have that conversation. Especially since she blamed him for her sister's addiction, as well as her pointless death.

Pushing the unwelcome memories aside, she concentrated on Hrebec. His heavily muscled back was just as spectacular as his front. When he'd whipped off his shirt, she'd felt a sudden, unexpected urge to touch all of those big, hard muscles. Without his shirt, she could see he had an intriguing raised texture covering his skin in a pattern of small dots. What would that feel like against her own skin, she wondered, and immediately tried to dismiss the thought.

His tight uniform pants showcased strong, muscular legs and a very impressive ass, but his tail fascinated her the most. It emerged just above the low waistband of his pants, wider at the base, then narrowing gradually until it wasn't more than two fingers wide at the tip. It too had a raised texture, and she had a sudden and very dirty thought.

As if aware of her thoughts, his tail rose and flicked in her direction, brushing against her wrist before dropping back behind him. From the sudden tension in his shoulders, she suspected Hrebec was aware of the movement.

The corridor emerged into a larger open space stacked with containers. On one side, two of Hrebec's men stacked three white boxes that bore a disturbing resemblance to coffins.

Without thinking, she grabbed his arm. "What are those?"

Hrebec paused to let her come up beside him. "Some of the Vedeckians decided to object to our boarding."

"Oh." She swallowed hard. "What about the rest of them?"

"They are already in the brig on board the *Defiance*."

"There was one—Kwaret—who wasn't as bad as the others. Do you know if he is alive?"

"You care for this male?" He frowned and his tail swished.

"No, of course not. But he did try to help us." The forbidding face showed no signs of relenting. "He was the one who made it possible for me to feed Tiana. And he may know where she came from."

"I will question him."

His words didn't reassure her at all.

"Listen, if it weren't for him, there's a good chance that Tiana would be dead, and possibly the rest of our children. Just keep that in mind."

"Very well," he said reluctantly.

They stopped in front of a closed hatch. Through a glass porthole, she could see a tube with another hatch at the end.

"Do you have any experience with zero gravity?" he asked.

"Do I look like an astronaut?" At his puzzled look, she sighed and shook her head. "No."

"Will you permit me to assist you?"

Not at all sure it was a good idea, she nodded slowly. "Yes."

"I am honored. Hold on to the infant."

He opened the door and, with a deft move, lifted her against his chest on the opposite side from Lucie. He was so big and warm that she felt safe and protected in his arms. A subtle citrus scent surrounded her and she suddenly wished she wasn't wearing her sweater so that she could get closer to him. He pushed through the hatch and her head spun as gravity disappeared. Still keeping her and Lucie tucked against his chest, he moved them through the tube with a few quick flicks of his tail. They were through the second hatch within seconds, and he set her down in front of him. Before she could step back, his tail reached out, wrapping around her waist and pressing her against his body. She was acutely conscious of a very hard ridge against her stomach.

Hrebec released her immediately and she stepped back, her cheeks flaming. *Don't look, don't look.* But it was impossible to resist and her gaze dropped to his very obvious—and very large—erection. Her eyes flashed to his face and he looked as embarrassed as she felt.

"I apologize," he said stiffly.

"Just try to keep that thing under control," she said, even though her nipples had tightened into hard points and there was an aching awareness between her legs she hadn't felt in a long time. Of all times for her suppressed sexuality to emerge, it had to be with a massive green alien...

The others followed them through the tunnel and she

welcomed the distraction. Mekoi, of course, assisted TeShawna and Vanessa, and both of them emerged with flushed faces. The rest came through quickly, except for Molly, who she could hear asking about Ribel. Abby came close to handing Tiana over to TeShawna and going back to fetch the foolish girl herself when she emerged from the tunnel. Only the sight of Molly's woebegone face made her bite her tongue.

"If you will follow me," Mekoi said, "I will see about providing the suitable equipment for the infants."

"Equipment, huh?" TeShawna raised an eyebrow and ran an entirely too suggestive look down Mekoi's body as his tail lashed.

Abby prayed she hadn't been as blatant when checking out Hrebec.

"Let's go, girls," she said firmly.

TeShawna winked at her, but they all obediently turned to follow Mekoi. Before she could join them, Hrebec's tail touched her arm very briefly. When she frowned at him, he nodded at Lucie.

"Abigail Wentworth, the little one is asleep. Would you care to put her to bed first?"

She hesitated, watching after the girls as they disappeared down a long grey corridor then looking back at her daughter, who was lying limp against Hrebec's massive shoulder.

"I suppose that makes sense. Lead on, Macduff."

"My name is Hrebec."

"It's a quote from—never mind. Lead on, Hrebec."

Instead of following the girls, he turned to the right and took her up a small flight of stairs. They opened onto a small landing. To one side, she could see what looked like a meeting room. Two doors lined the other side.

"Lieutenant Jedan and I are the only ones who have cabins up here. She will not be disturbed," he said as he approached one of the doors.

"Wait a minute. Your cabin?"

"It is the largest one. I thought it would be best since you have two children."

Before she could protest, he opened the door panel into what looked like an office. Like the rest of the ship, the room had grey metal walls and flooring, but the furnishings gave it a more personal feeling. A gorgeous wooden desk, polished wood gleaming in the dim light, dominated one side of the room, with an array of cabinets behind it. On the other wall was a small couch and a set of shelves with an assortment of colorful objects.

Hrebec opened a door panel at the rear of the room to reveal a surprisingly large bedroom. Of course, it needed to be large in order to accommodate the massive bed. She had a sudden vision of Hrebec's big body sprawled across that enormous mattress and felt a return of that disturbing attraction. She could feel her cheeks heating but fortunately, Hrebec was preoccupied with laying Lucie in the center of the bed, and covering her with a blanket.

Her daughter looked so small, lying in the center of the big bed. She didn't want to leave her alone, but she needed to check on the other girls and the shirt wrapped around Tiana felt suspiciously damp.

"Do you have a monitor?" she asked. "So I can hear if she wakes up?"

He rubbed the back of his neck, looking thoughtful, and then disappeared back into the office, returning with two bracelet-like devices. He placed one next to the bed. "These are communicators. I have set this one to transmit so you will be able to hear through the other one if she calls out."

"Thank you." She tried to put the device around her wrist but couldn't figure out how to fasten it. Hrebec took over, his big fingers warm and a little rough against her skin.

"Your wrists are so delicate and small," he said softly, and she was suddenly acutely aware of how close they were standing, his subtle citrusy scent washing over her again. His tail came up to circle her other wrist, just as he stepped back. With an oddly resigned look, he flicked it away and gestured to the door. "Come, Abigail Wentworth. Let us take care of the small one."

As Abby turned to follow him, she abruptly realized just how nice it felt to have someone helping her with her daughters.

Chapter Eight

Hrebec led the way to the medical bay, trying his best to keep his wayward tail under control. His thoughts were just as unruly, disrupting his usual weary resignation. While he would admit that he was certainly attracted to this human, with her fierceness and her determination, the fact that his tail was acting as if she were a potential mate was exceptionally disturbing. He had to remind himself that they were going to return the women to their planet, just as he had promised. Ignoring the surprising ache that caused in his chest, he led the way towards the sick bay.

A group of his men blocked the doorway, all peering in eagerly at the human females. "Gentlemen, return to your duties. Now."

Obviously reluctant, they obeyed. When he and Abigail finally entered the room, he sighed when he saw Ribel at the other end, once more in close contact with the young pregnant female. The girl didn't look much stronger than she had earlier so he decided to let Ribel remain. Jedan was there as well, still holding the infant with the bright red hair.

The girls had gathered around a central table to listen to Mekoi explain the absorbent bandages. He unwrapped the uniform shirt from around one of the infants. Unfortunately, he had chosen the male child, and as soon as the shirt was removed, the child urinated in a great arc that hit Mekoi directly in the face. There was a moment of shocked silence, and then everyone erupted in laughter.

Even Mekoi grinned ruefully as he shook his head and wiped his face. "I'm afraid that's not the first time that's happened. The negative part of being a medic."

Hrebec saw TeShawna give Mekoi a contemplative look before turning her attention to the rest of the demonstration. All of the girls, except the youngest one, took turns washing and wrapping the babies. Jedan took care of the red-headed child while Elaina watched approvingly.

When it was Abigail's turn, the tender care she took with the tiny Cire infant made his chest ache again. Once the child was changed, Abigail picked her up and cradled her while she surveyed the girls. He followed her gaze and realized they were all starting to droop with fatigue.

"What are the sleeping arrangements?" she asked him quietly, not entirely masking the suspicion in her eyes.

"Everyone volunteered, of course, but I asked the men to vacate the four forward cabins," Ribel said, stepping forward. "If that meets with your approval, sir."

It was an excellent suggestion. The four cabins were grouped together to one side of the stairs and would provide some privacy. He would arrange for a man to be stationed at the corridor, to prevent his men's curiosity from leading them astray. After a brief explanation to Abigail, he led the way to the rooms. Each of the small cabins was equipped with two beds.

"Amber, you and Molly should share a room," Abigail said firmly, shepherding them into the room farthest away from the stairs. "That way you'll have someone on hand in case you go into labor."

Molly gave Ribel a longing look but obeyed and entered the room, followed by the other pregnant girl who carried an infant. Each of the other girls quickly picked a room.

"You'd better give Ginger to me," Elaina told Jedan.

"She'll be hungry when she wakes up."

His lieutenant reluctantly handed over the red-headed infant, his tail reaching out to stroke Elaina's arm briefly. "You are very strong to take on the care of two infants. Is there anything I can do to assist you?"

The girl's speckled face turned pink again, and she gave a nervous laugh. "Not unless you wanna help change them bandage things."

"I would be honored."

The pink deepened but she didn't look away.

Abigail watched the exchange warily. "Maybe I should stay here with my girls."

"My men will behave," he assured her, but her words caught his attention and he realized he might have made an incorrect assumption. He had assumed that Lucie was her only child, but she had called all of the young females hers. Was it possible that she meant that these were all her children?

"These are all your girls?" he asked.

"Yes." She gave him a puzzled look.

"Your children?"

"Well, I suppose in a sense—wait a minute. Are you asking if I'm their mother?"

"Are you not?"

A feeling of relief shot through him as she slowly shook her head, immediately followed by the feeling that he had made a mistake as her eyes narrowed. Without another word, she turned around and stalked off. The other girls had been watching the exchange from the doors of their cabins and he was aware of a sudden silence.

"You fucked up now, boss," TeShawna said, and rolled her eyes.

"What did I do?" he asked, before he could restrain

himself.

"Don't you know nothing about women? Even if you thought she was old enough to have five grown children, you shouldn't have said it." She shook her head. "You better go apologize."

"It was only a question," he protested.

"And if someone asked you if you were too old to drive this ship, I bet you'd be pissed. Even if it was only a question."

The female's words rang uncomfortably true. He glanced around at the other females and they all bore expressions of amusement or pity. Even Jedan shook his head.

"Go on now," Elaina said sympathetically.

"Take her a present," Cassie advised. Hrebec cursed under his breath. After ordering Jedan to arrange for a guard, he headed off after Abigail.

When he entered his quarters, the door to the bedroom was open and he could see her bending over the bed to put the infant next to the older child, surrounded by pillows. The position drew her pants tightly across her luscious ass, and he couldn't help but envision taking her in that position, his cock sinking deep into her undoubtedly succulent cunt while all that warm, soft flesh cradled his body. His shaft responded to the image but he forced it away. They didn't even know if these human females had a similar physiology.

Then she turned around and his efforts at logic disappeared. She had shed her outer garment, leaving her in a tight pink top with thin straps cut low across spectacular breasts. She gasped at the sight of him and the quick breath had the tempting mounds threatening to overflow. His cock went to instant, aching fullness and his tail lashed.

"What are you..."

Her startled gaze dropped from his face to his groin and he had to bite back a groan as he saw her nipples harden.

"I, uh, came to apologize."

"I see." With a glance over her shoulder, she stepped into the front room with him and closed the door panel. "Why?"

"I am afraid that I hurt your feelings, and that was never my intention."

She sighed. "No, I know it wasn't. I overreacted. It is technically possible that I could be the mother of any one of them. They're all so young, especially Molly. Please make sure that your officer knows that. She is not of legal age in our society."

Her words didn't make sense to him. "I don't understand. If she's not of age, how did she become pregnant?"

"Because she trusted someone who took advantage of her."

Horror filled him. "Someone took advantage of a female? A young female?"

"Yes." She sighed. "All of the girls ended up with me because they were let down by the people in their lives, especially the men."

"Including you?"

Her eyes shifted away from him. "I suppose so. My... partner left because he didn't want to have to worry about a child interfering with his plans."

"He didn't want a child?" The thought was inconceivable.

"That never happens to the females in your society?"

He bowed his head, the bitter truth washing over him once again. "There are no females in our society."

Abby's mouth dropped open, too stunned to respond. Hrebec studied her face, then walked over to one of the cabinets, opening it to reveal a small bar area. He returned with a bottle and two small glasses.

"Would you like a drink?"

"Is that alcoholic?"

"Definitely." A smile split his face for the first time, and despite the strangeness of his features, it was oddly appealing and she couldn't help smiling back.

"I think a drink would be very nice."

He poured her a drink then gestured to the couch. It wasn't a very large piece of furniture and as soon as he sat down next to her, she was conscious of the heat of his body and that subtle citrus fragrance. Only one small lamp lit the room and the dimness made it feel more intimate, sitting close to him in the dark. She took a cautious sip of the liquor. It had a sweet, fiery taste, not unlike cinnamon, and left a trail of warmth down into her stomach.

"Is drinking allowed on military vessels?" she asked, trying for a lighter tone.

"This isn't exactly a military vessel."

Alarm spiked through her veins. Had this all been a ploy to get them on board and helpless? "What do you mean? You said you represented some planet thing."

"We do," he said quickly. "We represent the Confederated Planets. But we are part of the Interplanetary Reserve—we are volunteers, rather than a regular military patrol. I purchased this ship when I... left my planet."

Her curiosity returned, even though she had seen the

pain on his face. "Was that because you have no women there?" she asked cautiously.

"Yes." He tipped up his glass and drained it, then refilled both of theirs. "The Confederation was hit by a terrible disease when I was a child. We called it the Red Death, and it raged for many years on many planets. We eradicated it eventually, but the damage was enormous. Billions of people killed on almost every planet. It hit Ciresia especially hard. Not only did many of our men die, but all of our females were taken from us. It destroyed not only our present, but our future as well."

He drained his glass again, then stood up and paced restlessly. "We tried so many things. We even attempted to use artificial wombs and incubators like those the Vedeckians have on their ship. Our scientists are still trying, even though only a fraction of the infants have survived. All of the survivors have been male. Ensign Ribel is one of those few, along with most of my crew."

She stared at him for a moment and then poured herself another drink with a shaking hand, trying to imagine such a horrific event. Hrebec stopped pacing and leaned against the big wooden desk, a look of weary resignation on his face.

"Tiana is female," she said gently. "Perhaps there are others like her."

"We have searched to no avail. I pray the Vedeckians will provide more information."

"The ones who took us—" she started tentatively.

"The Vedeckians."

"—They called the girls breeders. Kwaret said they would be valuable. Is that because of this Red Death?"

"Yes. There are still many desperate races out there. We are one of them."

"You would buy females?"

"Never," he said immediately.

"Have you tried, um, mating with other races?" She knew her cheeks were turning pink but the liquor gave her courage. She downed her glass and poured him another while she waited for him to reply.

"No. We Cires consider ourselves unique and there was a fear that we would lose our identity if we mixed with other species." He contemplated his glass. "The High Council is still opposed. Of course, that did not stop some from attempting to violate that prohibition, especially when it became clear that none of our females would survive. However, it turned out to be more difficult than anticipated. The population of many other planets was decimated. Most races are still concentrating on restoring their own populations. And…"

"And what?" she prompted, when he paused.

"Many races are not physically compatible with us."

Chapter Nine

Despite Abby's best efforts, her eyes dropped to his groin. The rigid bar of flesh she'd detected earlier had seemed normal enough, if exceptionally large. Emboldened by the liquor, she asked. "Why not?"

"A female would be required to allow my cock inside her cunt," he said.

Her cheeks flamed at the blunt words and she pressed her thighs together. The thought of that large cock entering her was both exciting and a little intimidating.

"Um, isn't that the way it's normally done?" she asked.

He shook his head, sitting down next to her once more. "It is less common than you would expect. There are many ways of mating." Black eyes glowed at her. "Do you have a cunt capable of accepting a cock, Abigail?"

"Yes," she whispered. "Is that all?"

"No. My... a cock would have to knot inside her and remain locked there after ejaculation while my tail brought the female to climax. Could a human female handle that?"

The flush on her cheeks had spread down across her chest, her nipples were diamond hard, and there was a slow pulsating ache between her thighs. She didn't know if it was the frank discussion, the liquor, or the inevitable effect of a very large, very masculine body so close to hers for the first time in three years.

His eyes had traveled down over her chest, and he reached out, tracing a curious finger over the outline of the bat on her tank top and leaving a trail of fire where it passed.

"What is this creature?"

"It's called a bat," she said breathlessly. "It's a flying

animal."

"Is it the symbol of your clan?"

"It represents a hero. Someone who fought for justice," she managed to say, even though her whole body was concentrated on where he was still tracing the design on her shirt with a fascinated look on his face.

"Do you mind me touching you? It has been a long time since I felt the softness of a woman's body. And never one so enticing." His tail came up and wrapped around her wrist, just as he stroked a thumb across her nipple. A streak of pleasure went directly to her clit.

"N-no. I don't mind. It's been a long time for me as well."

"You are not mated?"

He eased the straps down over her shoulders, those rough, warm fingers caressing her, but she retained enough focus to frown.

"If I were, I wouldn't be doing this."

"I apologize. Of course you would not. It's just hard to believe that so desirable a female is not taken," he whispered against her shoulder. He followed his words with a kiss to the sensitive flesh, slowly kissing his way up her neck before raising his head. "I wish to kiss you."

She looked up into that strange alien face, so dissimilar from her own, but despite their differences, she felt inexplicably drawn to this man. Her senses swam with his heady, citrusy scent.

"Yes," she whispered.

His head descended, his mouth meeting hers with a confidence she hadn't expected, demanding a response from her. She gasped, and his tongue invaded her, his taste wild and tangy. Her hands instinctively went to his head, stroking over the hard ridges before clinging to his broad shoulders as the kiss intensified. He groaned and pressed her down into the couch, the raised texture of his skin rubbing against her nipples and sending shivers of excitement down her spine. She automatically parted her legs and his cock landed right where she needed it the most, against her aching clit. He put a hand under her ass, lifting her against him as she writhed. There was a sudden sharp tug on her nipple and sparks of light filled her vision as her body convulsed. She cried out into his mouth as he kept kissing her, stroking her ass, her face, her nipple...

The realization that he couldn't be touching her in three places at once finally penetrated her dazed pleasure and she pulled back a fraction, enough to look down her body and see his tail still wrapped around her nipple. The sight was both disturbing and curiously erotic, but it made her brain kick back on. What was she doing? Making out on a couch with an alien she barely knew? Never mind that so far he had shown himself to be thoughtful, kind, and protective. She knew better—although looking at those strange features watching her so intently, she desperately wanted to trust him.

"We should stop," she said, hating the shakiness in her voice.

He swallowed thickly. "Yes. You're right. Of course."

They stared at each other but he didn't raise his body and she didn't attempt to move.

"You should rest," he said finally, his voice sounding rough.

'What about you? Where are you going to sleep?" she asked.

"There is another couch in my ready room. I'll sleep there tonight and make other arrangements in the morning."

"Is it any bigger than this couch?"

"Not much," he admitted.

She took a deep breath. "Why don't you just stay here? That bed is certainly big enough. But no hanky panky," she added quickly. "The girls will be there."

He tilted his head. "Hankee pankee?"

Her cheeks heated. "What we were just doing."

"I liked the hankee pankee very much." His dark eyes roved over her appreciatively.

"So did I," she said shyly.

He finally sat up and pulled her up with him. Giving him a sideways glance, she caught the briefest glimpse of a large green head before he tucked his cock away with a wince.

"I'm sorry that you weren't, um, satisfied," she said. John would have been pouting and complaining by now.

"I found your pleasure very satisfying," he assured her and, despite her past experiences, she believed him.

She found she really wanted to tell him that she would return the favor, but instead she bit her lip and rose to her feet. "Let's go to bed."

Hrebec awoke after far too little sleep to find Lucie standing next to the bed staring at him. When he had followed Abigail into his room earlier, she had taken one side of the bed, next to Lucie, and he had taken the side next to Tiana. There was plenty of room—the oversized mattress was one of the few luxuries he had brought aboard the ship —but somehow, during the night, he had found himself with the infant on his chest, Lucie's knee digging into his stomach, and Abigail a soft warmth against his side. For a long time, he had lain there and allowed himself to imagine that this was his family and he had fought off sleep for as long as possible to relish the illusion.

"Leonardo," Lucie whispered, drawing him back from the memory.

"What is it, little one?" He made no attempt to correct his name, liking the fact that it was just between them.

"I losts my ball."

"Where did you see it last?"

"It ran away," she said innocently, but she bit her lip.

"Do you want me to find it for you?"

"Yes, please."

With a muffled sigh, he prepared to leave the haven of the bed, reluctantly unwrapping his tail from around Abigail's waist. Tiana still slept soundly on his chest, so he gently placed her next to Abigail. He admired the two of them together - the one so tiny and innocent and the other so lush and seductive.

"Leonardo," Lucie urged.

"I'm coming." He hadn't bothered to undress last night, so all he did now was pull on his boots.

The door into his office was already open and when he entered, he saw the outer door was as well. He must have forgotten to lock it in the sheer ecstasy of bringing Abigail to climax.

"Did you leave these rooms?" he asked sternly.

"Not 'xactly."

When he crossed to the door, he saw that the door to his ready room was also open.

"The ball runned over there." Lucie pointed.

He debated having a conversation with her about the fact that doors did not open themselves but in the end he simply nodded. "Then let's go find it."

The missing ball turned out to be hidden under one of the cabinets. He used his tail to retrieve it and was just returning it to Lucie when Abigail's voice sounded from across the hall.

"Lucinda Kathryn Reynolds."

"Uh oh. Mama is using all my names. That means she's mad." The child did not look particularly concerned. "Do you have more than one name?"

"My full name is Hrebec Zarmutek Nak'Charen."

"Wow! Did your mama use all your names when she was mad too?"

His mother had died when he was three, one of the first victims to fall prey to the disease that would eventually take all of their females, but he looked down at the trusting little face and could not bring himself to tell her. Neither could he lie to her.

"I don't remember, but it would not surprise me if she had."

Abigail's voice came again, a little more frantic this time.

"You should return to your mother."

"Okay." She gave him a sunny smile and curled her impossibly tiny fingers around one of his. "Will you take me? So you can 'splain about the ball?"

The trust on her face and the warmth of her touch rocketed through him and in that moment, Hrebec Zarmutek Nak'Charen lost his heart completely. "I will take you wherever you wish."

It was a vow.

Chapter Ten

H rebec passed Lucie off to Abigail, who received her daughter with a tight embrace and a stern warning to not wander off again.

"I will show you how to lock the doors," he said. "I apologize for my distraction last night."

As she looked up at him, the intriguing pink color highlighted her cheeks, and he suspected that she remembered why he had been so distracted. Unfortunately, she had donned her outer garment once more, but he could visualize all too clearly how that heated color had spread down across her chest and over her luscious breasts. His cock started to thicken, his tail already reaching for her, but he forced his body under control.

"If it would not inconvenience you, I would like to refresh myself and put on a clean uniform."

"Oh, no. Of course not. This is your cabin, after all."

"Does we live with you now, Leonardo?" Lucie asked, and he had to fight the overwhelming urge to tell her yes.

"It's just temporary, baby," Abigail said. "The captain is going to take us back to our house on Earth."

The child's bottom lip poked out. "I wants to stay with Leonardo."

Abigail looked to him, seeking a support that he did not want to give, so he took the coward's way out by gathering his clothes and disappearing into the bathroom. When he emerged, Lucie was still pouting, and Abigail paced the length of the room, rocking Tiana while the child made little whimpering cries.

"I need a bottle for her," she said urgently. "I didn't

realize how little was left in the one I had."

"Bottle?"

"It's to feed her with. I need more formula."

"You mean a nutritional substance?" His thoughts flashed back to the hundreds of combinations they had tried in the past and his heart sank. What if they were no more successful with this precious infant?

"Yes." She looked at him anxiously. "Can you ask Doctor Mekoi?"

"Of course." After a brief conversation over his communicator with the medic, he rubbed the back of his neck, then turned to Abigail. "Mekoi is not sure what would be best. The nutritional substances we used before were frequently unsuccessful." At her appalled look, he hurried on. "He will prepare a selection for you to try."

"Whatever Kwaret was giving her seemed to be fine. Can't we just use that?"

"Do you know what it contained?"

"Of course not." Tiana's whimpers grew in frequency and Abigail rocked her soothingly. "It was grey. That's all I know. Why don't you ask him?"

His pride rebelled against the idea of asking a Vedeckian slave trafficker for assistance, but the infant's health was far more important. Turning back to the communication panel, he ordered the one called Kwaret to be brought to the medical bay.

"We will meet him there," he told her.

"Lucie, do you want to go play with the girls?"

"No. I wanna stay with Leonardo."

He went down on one knee before her, his tail wrapping around her small waist. "I have work to do, little one. If your mother permits, I will join you for the mid-shift meal."

When he glanced at Abigail, seeking her input, she blushed again and bit her lip. That heated shade of pink was fast becoming his favorite color.

"That would be very nice," she said.

"But for now, you will spend time with the females while we try to help Tiana," he told Lucie, his tone firm but gentle.

She gave a reluctant nod, then patted his tail, and jumped up, her smile restored. "I's ready!"

Abby followed Hrebec to the lab. Kwaret was already there, standing off to one side, wringing his cuffed hands and shooting anxious looks at his guard. The burly Cire made the tall, thin Vedeckian appear weak and fragile.

"Is it really necessary to cuff him?" Abby muttered to Hrebec. "Do you really think he can get past your guard, let alone the rest of you?"

"He is a prisoner," he said sternly, but then relented. "Very well. Cuvar, release his hands." He looked at Kwaret and his voice turned deadly. "Vedeckian, be assured that if you make any attempt to escape, you will be severely punished."

"Y-yes, Captain," Kwaret stuttered.

Abby couldn't blame him. Hrebec was an intimidating sight in full warrior mode.

Hrebec gestured to Tiana. "We wish to know what nutritional substance was given to the infant."

Kwaret rubbed his wrists. "It was a standard formula, enhanced for Cire physiology."

"Like one of these?" Mekoi asked, showing him a screen with what looked like utter gobbledygook to Abby.

"Yes, that one. The third one down."

Mekoi shook his head, glancing at Hrebec. "We tried that one before. It didn't work."

"Well, it was working for Tiana," Abby said. The baby was starting to go quiet again, which worried her even more than the pitiful whimpers. "Can you make it?"

"Yes. I have the requirements," Mekoi said.

Within a few minutes, he and Kwaret had produced a bottle of the grey fluid.

"Can you heat it a little?" she asked.

"Heat?" Mekoi asked.

"Good lord, don't you people know anything about babies? Yes, heat it to the temperature it would be if it came from her mother."

Mekoi put the bottle in a device that looked startlingly like an Earth microwave and pulled it back out immediately. "Here."

The milk was the perfect temperature. She dribbled a little bit on Tiana's mouth and finally coaxed her into accepting the bottle. As soon as her lips closed around it, she sucked eagerly. Everyone in the room, even Kwaret, breathed a sigh of relief.

"Now, Vedeckian," Hrebec said, looming over the smaller man. "Tell us where she came from."

Kwaret looked around nervously, but began talking readily enough. "We stopped on Trevelor for supplies to outfit the, um, lab. I was at the hospital completing the transaction when a Cire female was brought in. She was in labor and she died after giving birth to the infant." He looked at Tiana, now sucking happily on her bottle. "I didn't know what else to do, so I purchased the child. Commander Khaen was not pleased."

"They let you buy her?" Hrebec asked, his face stiff with anger.

Kwaret shrank back, but he kept talking. "I don't think they knew what else to do with her. The Trevelorians are a very different species."

"And the female had no family?" Hrebec's eyes were focused on Kwaret.

"Since she came in alone, the hospital didn't know and they didn't have time to investigate. There was an outbreak of some kind of disease at the same time. Someone mentioned that she was headed for the spaceport, but I think that was only speculation." He looked around at his audience and gave a helpless little shrug. "I swear that's all I know."

"Are you sure they said heading to the spaceport? Not coming from it?"

"I think so. Does it matter?"

"If she was living on the planet, there could be more Cires there," Hrebec said slowly, exchanging a look with Mekoi.

"Many people fled when the plague was escalating." The medic shook his head, the same look of resignation on his face that Abby had seen on Hrebec's the previous night. "They didn't know that it was pointless. Perhaps some ended up on Trevelor. I'm not familiar with the location."

"It's a small planet," Kwaret volunteered. "Sparsely populated even before the Red Death, but they didn't seem as affected as many of the other planets in the Confederation. Their dyes are highly desirable. You should see some of the fabric that can be created—" He broke off, looking embarrassed. "Forgive me. I realize that trading opportunities are not of interest to you."

Hrebec didn't appear to have been listening. Instead, he frowned thoughtfully at Mekoi. "We should see if there are any records available on Ciresia. It's unlikely, given the chaos of the times, but it's possible."

"Yes, sir."

Hrebec gave Kwaret a stiff nod. "Thank you for your assistance, Vedeckian."

"His name is Kwaret," Abby said impatiently. "But there's one thing I don't understand, Kwaret. How did you keep Tiana alive if she wouldn't eat?"

"I was giving her injections of vitamins and nutrients, but since Commander Khaen did not approve, I had limited opportunities to do so. He said that if she couldn't thrive on the standard nutrition, that no one would be willing to purchase her." He shot a nervous glance at the Cires. "He also wasn't sure if there was a market for her, since you have a reputation for being um, law-abiding, and he wasn't sure what her value would be elsewhere."

"I can't believe she survived," Abby said, tucking the baby closer.

"I had my doubts. I was only able to get her to take the nutrition once."

"But you were successful one time. How?" Mekoi asked.

"I don't know. I was giving her an injection when the automated feeding began and she actually took some sustenance."

A light clicked on in Abby's brain. "Were you holding her?"

"Yes, I believe so."

"Of course. All babies need to be held, but maybe it's an actual physical requirement for a Cire baby." She looked at Hrebec. "You said you tried to raise babies. Were they also in labs like the one on the ship?"

"Yes. Do you really think it would make a difference?"

"I don't know. I am basing this on a data set of one baby. But you said they were still trying. Can you ask them to try again, this time holding the babies during feeding? And tell them to heat the formula?"

Hrebec and Mekoi stared at each other, an almost reluctant look of hope on their faces.

"Could it really be that simple?" Hrebec asked.

"It seems unlikely the solution will be that simple, but I will communicate our recommendations immediately," Mekoi said slowly, then slanted a glance at Tiana. "She will be a good point of comparison."

Abby didn't like the speculation on his face, and gathered the now sleeping baby closer. "She's a baby—she's not some damn lab rat you can study."

He looked horrified. "No, of course not. I just meant that the fact that she is thriving would help to establish the validity of our theory—"

Before he could finish, there was a loud disruption from the corridor and Abby went on alert as she recognized TeShawna's voice. "What the fuck do you think you're doing?"

Mama and the Alien Warrior

Chapter Eleven

Abby rushed out of the lab, not entirely surprised that both Mekoi and Hrebec followed immediately. Through the large crowd of aliens gathered in the small area, she could just make out TeShawna standing at the foot of the stairs, her hands on her hips.

Beside her, Mekoi growled, the sound harsh enough to make her pull away, backing right into Hrebec. His arms and his tail both wrapped around her for a moment before he let out a roar of his own, the sound loud enough to startle Tiana awake. Instead of crying, the baby's eyes fastened on Hrebec and she gave her wide toothless grin.

"Attention!" Hrebec snapped as the men turned cowed faces in his direction.

The crowd in the corridor separated immediately and fell into place along the walls. Now that they were lined up, she could see that there were less of them than she had originally thought. Mekoi immediately started to head for TeShawna, but he took one look at Hrebec and stepped back.

"Stay with the Vedeckian," Hrebec ordered the guard, gesturing for Abby to go ahead of him.

TeShawna waited at the far end of the corridor, her hands still on her hips. A flustered guard stood next to her.

"What's the matter, TeShawna?" Abby asked.

"They're keeping us fucking prisoner," the girl snapped. "I was just trying to go to the med lab to get some more of those bandage things." She snuck a look at Mekoi, and Abby suspected that procuring diapers hadn't been her only motivation. "And there was a whole damn crowd of them out here, peering at me like I'm some kind of damn exhibit! This jerk wouldn't let me go any further."

"Captain, I just wanted the female to wait while I cleared the corridor," the guard said anxiously.

"What are they all doing here?" Abby demanded.

Hrebec sighed and rubbed his eyes, looking tired all of a sudden. A pang of guilt shot through her as she remembered that he'd had a late and interrupted night, even before they had taken his bed. Not that he had seemed to mind sharing it. She'd actually been a little disappointed when she woke up alone... but that wasn't something she wanted to think about right now, and she forced her attention back to the present situation.

Hrebec leaned closer and lowered his voice. "Most of them have rarely seen a female, let alone a child. They are curious but they mean no harm."

"Never seen? Oh." As she looked at the crewmen lining the walls, she realized that despite their size, they tended to have the same smooth complexions and unmarked skin as the young ensign. She sighed. "I think I understand, but the girls aren't a show for them to watch. They need to stay away. And the girls should be free to leave their cabins."

"Damn right we should," TeShawna added, but Abby could tell that she'd lost some of her fire with Hrebec's words.

Hrebec turned to the crew. "Since all of you have so much time on your hands, report to the training room. I expect you to have performed ten circuits before I join you. We'll see how much energy you have left when you face me." He bared his teeth. The crewmen paled noticeably, turning various sickly shades of green. "Dismissed."

The young warriors took off at a run. Hrebec sighed and turned back to Abby.

"I will take care of it," he said. "But if the females are

free to roam the ship, they will encounter the crew. Perhaps it would be best if we introduced them?"

"Maybe," she said tentatively. It did make a certain amount of sense. "How many are on the ship?"

"Twenty-four." Sorrow flashed across his face. "We didn't have many to choose from."

"Perhaps a communal meal would be nice? That would give everyone a chance to meet."

He rubbed the back of his neck. "That's not a bad idea. Perhaps half at the mid-shift meal and half this evening? The crew members who were here just now can wait until then."

She grinned at him. "You're an evil man."

He returned the smile, and for just a second, she could feel an almost palpable warmth flowing between them. Flustered, she dragged her eyes away and turned to TeShawna. The girl was frowning at Mekoi, who was very determinedly not looking at her, although Abby couldn't help but notice that his tail kept creeping in TeShawna's direction.

"TeShawna, why don't you get the rest of the girls and we'll all go back to the lab for more bandages?"

"Yeah, okay. And what about some food for us? I need to keep up my strength."

"You are hungry?" Mekoi looked appalled, his gaze whipping from the now vacant corridor directly to TeShawna.

"Well, yeah. Those Veckians, or whatever you called 'em, at least fed us regular."

"I am truly sorry for my thoughtlessness." In his agitation, he had forgotten to control his tail, and it was now patting TeShawna's wrist. She gave it a bemused look, but Abby noticed she didn't object. Somehow, Abby wasn't altogether surprised when Hrebec's tail wrapped around her own wrist briefly before he pulled it back.

"I will take you to the cook," Hrebec said. "You can advise him as to what would be most suitable for your females. I will have it served in my ready room so you will be undisturbed."

"Thank you, I—"

"Mama! You's been gone forever." Lucie appeared at the door of Cassie's cabin and immediately came flying towards her.

Since Abby still held Tiana, she braced herself, but Hrebec intercepted the small body and lifted Lucie up against his chest.

She gave him a sunny smile. "You's been gone forever, too."

"We were tending to your sister," he said gravely. A lump appeared in Abby's throat at his easy acceptance of her claim on both girls. "Your mother and I were about to arrange for a meal for the rest of you."

"Good. I's starving."

"It's just an expression," Abby said quickly as horror crossed his face and his tail came up to circle Lucie's waist. "Don't exaggerate, Lucie."

"But Mama, my tummy is empty," she said with a pitiful look.

"Then we must remedy that at once," Hrebec said, obviously impatient to feed her daughter.

Abby rolled her eyes but nodded. "Fine. TeShawna, please go get the other girls and take everybody to the lab for supplies. Then I'm sure that Mekoi can bring you to this ready room?"

"Of course."

"Dornic, you will accompany the females as well,"

Hrebec ordered. "If you begin to attract undue attention, contact me immediately."

"Yes, sir."

The words were hardly out of his mouth before Hrebec's tail was at Abby's waist, urging her gently but firmly towards the stairs.

"Make sure Molly goes with you!" Abby called over her shoulder before she gave in and let Hrebec take her away.

An hour later, Hrebec circled the young warrior in the ring, fighting the desire to return to Abigail and ensure that she and her daughters were adequately fed. He was still appalled that he had neglected to provide for their comfort. The fact that it had occurred because of the necessity of feeding the infant did not appease his conscience.

Taking advantage of his distraction, his opponent managed to get him in a partial hold. Hrebec cursed under his breath but forced himself to concentrate, sending the other man flying in three controlled moves. A soft gasp came from the entrance and he looked up to see Abigail and Lucie standing in the opening. A hush spread through the room.

Dismayed that the females might be upset by the violence of his actions, he flipped out of the ring and went to meet them. As he approached, he noticed that Abigail looked far from dismayed. She bit her lip and her eyes dropped down over his body. He realized that he was clad only in brief training shorts, as were the rest of his men. At her avid gaze, his shaft started to respond and he firmly forced it back under control. Since he did not want her looking at anyone else with the same degree of appreciation, he moved to block her view of the room.

Lucie bounced excitedly. "I knewed it. I knewed you was Leonardo."

He frowned at Abigail and she laughed. "Leonardo is a… superhero that she's seen on television. A fictional character."

The child thought of him as a hero? His shoulders stretched back with pride. "I am most honored."

"Can you teach me how to do that?" Lucie added.

"Females are not warriors." The very idea appalled him.

"Why not?" Abigail straightened at his words, and he had the distinct feeling that he had said something else to offend her.

"Because they are to be cherished, protected."

"A woman has to be able to protect herself."

"But that is a male's job. It is his honor and his privilege."

She gave a bitter laugh. "Yeah, well, sometimes no male is around to do the job." Her chin came up. "And even if he is, I want to stand next to him, not behind him."

A thousand objections rushed through his head, but he had gained enough wisdom not to utter them.

Sedlit was not so wise. The young ensign stepped forward eagerly. "A woman is not capable of violence. I would gladly stand between you and danger."

Hrebec growled and only just refrained from challenging Sedlit to step into the ring. The youngster thought he could have the privilege of defending Hrebec's woman?

Abigail's eyes narrowed. "I assure you, I am quite capable of violence." She turned back to Hrebec and huffed.

"What are you teaching these boys?"

Before he could attempt to defend himself, Lucie tugged on his hand. "Teach me too."

Gazing down at her eager little face, he could not find it within himself to refuse. "Of course, little one. But perhaps now is not the right time. Did you need me, Abigail?"

Her cheeks flushed that delightful pink color again and her eyes roved over his body a second time, causing his shaft to respond. "Um, yes. I wanted to speak to you about the journey back to Earth."

His arousal disappeared as if dashed with cold water. Of course. How could he have forgotten that he had promised to return her to her planet? He forced down his instinctive protest and gave a formal bow. "Very well. I will meet you in my office as soon as I have dressed."

"Thank you."

Mama and the Alien Warrior

Chapter Twelve

"Captain." Before Hrebec could return to his office, Lieutenant Jedan intercepted him.

Jedan was the one who had first put the thought of leaving Ciresia into Hrebec's head. Although they hadn't known each other well at the time, Jedan had worked for him as part of the security for the lab complex. He had come to report one day and found Hrebec staring at a memory eraser. The machine had been developed because of the high rates of suicides among the survivors. It allowed them to forget the past, to forget the pain and suffering endured by their loved ones; in some cases, they even chose to forget that their loved ones had ever existed.

"Sir, what are you doing?"

Hrebec hadn't answered at first, turning the device over and over in his hands. His father had just died and the experiments were still failing. Could he erase enough of his memory to be able to start over with the sense of optimism he had once experienced? Would there be anything left of what made him uniquely himself?

"Sir—Hrebec—I have another suggestion."

"Yes?" he asked finally, dragging his thoughts away from the past.

"You know that the Confederated Planets are recruiting volunteers for their Interplanetary Reserve?"

Frowning, he dropped the device and looked up at his head guard. "I had heard something to that effect, yes."

"If you were to outfit a ship and assemble a crew, you could leave Ciresia and join the Reserve."

Leave? His first reaction had been an immediate denial, but then he rose and went to the window, staring out at the long buildings holding the incubators... the useless incubators. And beyond them, the desolate buildings, the empty streets. For the first time in a very long time, he felt a flicker of interest, almost eagerness. He could do no more here.

Perhaps out there, he could make a difference.

In the end, he had made the decision to leave and purchased a ship. Jedan had been the first to volunteer for his crew and Hrebec had made him second-in-command.

Now Jedan stood at attention, waiting for a response.

"Yes, Lieutenant?"

"Sir, the Ciresian High Council has responded to our message regarding the suggestions to improve infant viability. They are most excited."

"I'm sure they are." He could only pray that this attempt did not result in the failure that had haunted all of their previous efforts. Impatient to get to Abigail, he started to turn away, but Jedan continued.

"There is more, sir. They... strongly suggested that we proceed to Trevelor immediately to see if there are additional Cire females on the planet. They will contact the Interplanetary Reserve to make sure they understand the importance of this mission and approve the exploration."

This was not good. While he was not directly under the authority of the Ciresian High Council, he had agreed to follow the orders given by Reserve headquarters.

"I made a commitment to the Earth females."

"Yes, sir. I did mention that. However, they suggested that another ship could perform that task. They also encouraged us to take possession of the infant as soon as possible."

"What?" He scowled at his lieutenant. "Do they understand that it is only because of Abigail that Tiana is even alive?"

"I don't know." Jedan looked grim and unhappy. "I believe they think that we have discovered the answer to the infants failing to thrive and they do not trust an alien female."

Anger roared through Hrebec with such ferocity that he drove his fist into the wall. The resulting pain was nothing to the pain in his heart.

"They would take a child from her mother?"

Jedan sighed and rubbed his face. "Hrebec, I understand. Abigail treats the child as tenderly as my female... as Elaina treats her son. But you know how desperate they are to restore Ciresia."

Of course he did. He had been part of the madness for many years. "But at what cost?"

The two men stared at each other, then Jedan asked, "What are you going to do?"

"I don't know. I need to talk to Abigail."

Abby paced the cabin impatiently. Lucie was visiting with the ship's cook, a grizzled old Cire with thick head ridges and dark markings denoting his age. When they had met Pravit earlier to go over food that would be palatable to the humans, Lucie had used big eyes and a pleading face to worm a variety of sweets from him. Concerned about the safety of the food, Abby had protested, but he had shown her a food analyzer that had already been programmed to human dietary requirements.

After their brief visit to the gym, Lucie had decided to go back and "help" Pravit with the mid-shift meal, and when Abby left her, she was happily seated on a high stool, regaling him with the story of her adventures. Now Tiana was napping peacefully in the big bed and Abby was once again going to be alone with Hrebec. She couldn't help but remember seeing him in the gym, muscles bulging as he threw the other Cire across the space with a few quick moves. For a man of his size, he moved with surprising agility.

Her breasts tingled, and she looked down to see her nipples straining against her tank top. She pulled on her cardigan and resolutely ignored the ache between her legs and her gathering excitement. He was coming to discuss plans for her return to Earth, not to satisfy her newly reawakened sexual urges. However, when he appeared at the door, she couldn't resist a hungry look at his body, once again covered—but not concealed—by the tight white uniform. When she got to his face, thoughts of sexual need disappeared. He looked stern and worried.

"Hrebec, is something wrong?"

He looked startled, then gestured for her to sit.

"How did you know?" he asked.

Because she could read his face already, despite his strange alien features. Before she could decide how to phrase that though, he continued speaking.

"We informed the Ciresian High Council of your suggestions about the nutritional supplement and how to feed the infants."

"Yes? Did they disagree?"

"No. In fact, they are excited." He paused, looked surprisingly hesitant. "We also informed them about Tiana and that a Cire female was on Trevelor. They want us to investigate."

"I can understand that. I'm sure they're very excited. But I don't see—"

"Immediately. They want us to take the ship there

now."

It took a moment for his words to sink in, and to her surprise, she wasn't quite as upset as she thought she would be. Nonetheless... "You promised to take us back."

"I know. Which leaves two alternatives. You can come with us to Trevelor while we investigate, and I will return you to Earth once the investigation is complete. If that is not satisfactory, I will arrange for another Confederated ship to make the journey."

"Would they be Cires also?"

"No." He looked conflicted, but finally added simply, "I'm sure they would be honorable men."

He didn't sound as convincing as Abby would have liked. She stared at him, her mind spinning as she considered the options. If it were up to her, she would rather stay with him, but she had to consider the girls. The girls...

"Does Doctor Mekoi have any training in childbirth?" she asked.

Hrebec slowly shook his head. "I doubt it. It has been many years since we have had a live birth on Ciresia."

"How far is Trevelor?"

"Approximately four days."

"And Earth?"

"At least fourteen days, per the information we retrieved from the Vedeckian ship."

She sighed. "Kwaret said that there was a hospital on Trevelor. I think it's best that we accompany you. Both Molly and Amber are due to give birth in the next week or so."

His face actually paled. "I will inform Mekoi at once. We will make whatever preparations we can." He moved over to his desk and sent a quick message before turning back to her. "There is something else."

"Yes?"

"Your people—they are accepting of outsiders?"

"That's an odd question." She frowned at him. "I suppose some are, and some aren't. Why?"

He stared at his hands, but he finally raised his head and looked at her, black eyes full of sorrow. "Tiana."

For a moment, she was puzzled, but then his meaning became clear and her hands started to shake. Of course. As much as she loved the little girl, she was an alien. How could she take her to a place where she would be treated as a curiosity, perhaps even as a lab experiment? A vision of E.T. dying in his bubble popped into her head and tears started to roll down her cheeks. Hrebec cursed, then he was next to her on the couch, lifting her onto his lap and letting her cry against his big warm chest, his tail curling around her waist as she gave in to her misery.

A very long time later, her tears finally eased and she scrubbed at her face with her sleeve. She felt limp with exhaustion and sorrow but she looked up at him. "What will become of her?"

"I thought, perhaps..." He hesitated for a long moment, staring across the room at his desk before his voice firmed. "I thought, perhaps, that I could adopt her."

"You?"

"Yes. Unless you object?"

Her first instinct was to give a bitter reply, but gazing at that strong, stiff face, she couldn't do it. "No, I don't object. You would make a wonderful father."

"You truly think so?"

She remembered how sweet and protective he already was, with both the baby and with Lucie, and nodded. "I do think so. And thank you for asking my opinion. If I can't be with her, then I would rather she was with you than with any—"

His head descended before she finished speaking, and he kissed her with a passionate intensity that had her responding instinctively, her hands curling into his shirt, wanting him closer. Her breasts rubbed against the wonderful texture of his chest and she was suddenly a needy, throbbing mess. His cock was a rigid bar under her butt and her mind flashed back to the previous night.

She slid off of his lap. His hands resisted for a second, his tail a fraction longer, and then he let her go. Instead of moving away, she went to her knees in front of him. His eyes widened as her hands moved to his pants. With shaking fingers, she began to unfasten them.

"Abigail, what are you doing?"

"Remembering last night." She wrestled with the pants and they suddenly parted. She had a brief glimpse of a very large, very erect, very green cock before his hand came down to cover it.

"I don't understand. Are you prepared to take my seed?"

Yes. No. She suppressed the flash of heat that scorched through her at the vision of that huge cock filling her. For right now, she only wanted to bring him pleasure and lose herself in giving him fulfillment.

"I want to taste you," she whispered, as she tugged at his hand.

"That is a forbidden—oh, Granthar."

Since he wouldn't move his hand, she slipped her tongue between his fingers and took a quick lick of hot, delicious—*nubbed?*—flesh. His resistance weakened as soon as he felt her tongue and she pried the rest of his fingers away to reveal his cock in all its glory. It was enormous, covered with the same raised nubs that covered his skin. The basic shape was similar to a human penis, but it had a wider, flatter head, and the shaft had a thicker section beneath the head and another, even thicker, at the base. Her fingers didn't quite meet around it but she grasped as much as she could and gave him a long, slow tug.

His whole body tensed, his hand grasping the arm of the couch so tightly she heard something crack. His tail twined around her upper body, reaching for her breasts. She let go of him long enough to tug off her sweater impatiently while she used her tongue to explore, the bumpy surface adding to her desire. As soon as the cardigan was out of the way, his tail immediately went to her breasts, dipping inside her tank to tug and squeeze her nipples, and she moaned with delight.

"Abigail, it is forbidden," he gasped.

His hand came to her head, but instead of pushing her away, he tightened his grip. She took hold of him again and positioned the wide head at her lips. He didn't have a single hole like a human male, but three narrow slits, already weeping precum. She licked experimentally, then sighed with pleasure. He tasted amazing, clean and citrusy, like a lemon ice on a hot summer day. She licked again, running her tongue along each slit as he groaned and his hand tightened in her hair.

Stretching her lips apart, she took the whole head into her mouth. It was a tight fit, but she loved feeling him quiver beneath her. She gave one gentle, experimental suck and he exploded. Crying her name in a hoarse voice, he held her in place as a fountain of cool lemony seed rushed over her tongue and down her throat. She swallowed eagerly, using her tongue to urge him on as he shuddered and jerked for an endless minute. When he finally stilled, she gave him one last gentle lick and raised her head to smile at him.

Instead of smiling back, his face was rigid, every muscle taut. He looked every inch an alien warrior, and before she could ask him what was wrong, he had lowered her to the floor. She heard a ripping sound and then her pants were gone.

"Hrebec, what are you doing?"

He bared his teeth. "My turn."

Mama and the Alien Warrior

Chapter Thirteen

P art of Hrebec knew that he should be horrified. He had committed a forbidden act—and enjoyed every second of it—and he was not treating his woman with the respect and dignity she deserved. However, that part was buried beneath the primitive male whose only focus at this moment was to satisfy his female. The maddening scent of her arousal filled the air, stronger now that he had removed the fabric barring his way. He spread her legs, feasting his eyes on the delights hidden between them: a small patch of dark curls guarding a silky pink slit. He parted them impatiently, revealing even more flushed, glistening flesh surrounding an impossibly tiny entrance and a small pearl of swollen flesh.

"What is this?" he growled and licked the impudent nub.

Her taste exploded in his mouth, sweet, tangy, delicious, and he licked again, eager for more. Her body arched upward and her hands reached for his head. Ah, a pleasure receptacle. He grasped her hips with both hands, pulling her closer as he searched for the best way to please her. He licked, circled, tugged, while she made indecipherable noises and tried to rise to meet him. His tail abandoned her luscious breasts and slipped between her legs, probing at the small entrance until she softened enough for it to slip inside.

"Oh, my god, what are you doing? Oh, that feels so good..."

Her channel was so tight that his tail could barely move, but he worked it deeper, until he found a spot that caused even more of her delicious wetness to surround him.

He stroked it repeatedly while he continued his attentions to her pleasure receptacle, sucking it into his mouth as she had taken him into hers. Her whole body seized, and then she cried out again, her delicious essence flooding his tongue. Her cunt convulsed around his tail so tightly that he could only imagine what it would feel like around his cock. The thought was enough. His shaft overflowed with a forbidden explosion of seed. He ground down against the soft carpet and wished it were her soft flesh instead.

As soon as the final jet left his body, his shaft stiffened again, already aching for more. He was almost blind with the need to push inside the tight fist of her cunt, to feel her channel lock around him as his knot expanded and he brought her to climax again and again. He rose over her, his cock already seeking her entrance, but just as he felt the kiss of her hot, wet flesh, her eyes opened. For a moment, he saw only willingness in her gaze, and he started to press against her, but then alarm replaced it and her hand came up.

"No, Hrebec. We can't."

Abby felt relief, and perhaps the tiniest bit of disappointment, when Hrebec froze at her words.

"You do not want this?" he asked, running that marvelous nubbed cock the length of her slit.

'We can't," she repeated. "I'm not on birth control."

His eyes heated even more and she suddenly realized how much that would encourage a man whose species teetered on the verge of extinction. His cock jerked against her clit, causing a spasm of pleasure so intense that she almost gave in. But she wasn't one of her reckless teenagers. She was an adult, and she had to be responsible.

"Please, Hrebec," she said softly.

With a muffled curse, he pulled back. To her surprise, he didn't stomp off, but instead, he sat back against the couch and lifted her up onto his lap. She could feel his rigid cock beneath her ass—did that thing ever go down? — but he made no attempt to resume his actions, simply wrapping his arms and tail around her. She sighed and nestled closer, feeling unexpectedly shaky from both her climax and the feelings rushing through her—feelings she did not want to examine too closely.

He stroked her hair, and she found herself petting his tail where it was wrapped around her. As her body began to relax, she thought back to what he had said.

"What did you mean by that—that it was forbidden?"

His body tensed, but he answered willingly enough. "It is forbidden to waste seed on any act that is not for the purpose of procreation."

"Is that a religious thing?" she asked, and then immediately felt silly. "No, of course not. It's because your race is…"

"Is dying. You can say it." He sighed and rested his cheek on her hair. "And you're right. As soon as we are capable, we are required to donate our seed every week."

"Every week? Do you, um, masturbate into a cup or something like that?"

"You mean touch ourselves? No. There is a machine." His voice tightened. "It is not pleasant, but I believe that is because they do not want to encourage us to seek pleasure on our own."

She knew her cheeks were turning pink, but thankfully her face was buried against his chest. Somehow that gave her the courage to ask the next question. "You already, um, ejaculated twice and you're still hard. Why are they so worried about wasting seed when you seem to have so much to spare?"

"It was not fertilized. Remember what I said last night? I would have to knot before my seed becomes fertile."

"So the machine..."

"Forces us to knot? Yes." His voice was still tight, and she stroked his tail comfortingly.

"But you no longer have to use those machines, right?"

"No. It is not viable to transport seed for any distance."

A sudden thought struck her. If there were no females on Ciresia and he was forbidden to have sex unless it was an attempt at procreation... She leaned back so that she could see his face.

"Hrebec, have you ever had sex?"

His cheeks darkened and he looked away. "I am ashamed to admit that I have. The first month after *Defiance* assumed its duties, we were at a trading port. There was a female there. After some discussion, we agreed that she was probably physically compatible."

A feeling that bore an uncomfortable resemblance to jealousy spread through her, but she tried to keep her voice calm. "Did you enjoy it?"

"No. She didn't feel right or smell right. I didn't knot and I felt uncomfortable and ashamed."

She bit her lip. "I'm sorry. I didn't want you to feel that way. I just wanted to give you pleasure."

"You did." His eyes heated. "You do feel right, Abigail. You smell delicious and you taste even better. I have no doubt that I would knot inside your tight little cunt."

A corresponding surge of lust shot through her but she pushed it firmly aside. "And that's why we can't have sex. What if I got pregnant? The odds are that it wouldn't happen. I'm older and less fertile and our species are most likely to be incompatible, but we can't take the risk. There's no future for us." Her words echoed the hollowness she felt inside, but before he could respond, Tiana cried out from the next room.

"Saved by the bell," she muttered.

He frowned at her. "There is no bell."

"It's an expression." She started to climb to her feet and he lifted her effortlessly. "Thank you. Where are my pants?"

She found them in a crumpled heap on the floor and could see the long rip up one leg where he had torn them off of her.

"Dammit, Hrebec. This is the only outfit I have. Can you find a way to fix them?"

Abandoning the useless garment, she headed for her daughter.

Abby fed and changed Tiana before emerging from the bedroom to find Hrebec waiting for her. To her surprise, he had actually mended her pants, the tear almost invisible.

"How did you do that?"

He showed her a device like a long metal wand and explained how it could be used to fuse together a number of materials, including most fabrics.

"It occurs to me that your females will need clothing for themselves and for the infants. I apologize for not thinking of this before. We have spare uniforms and I'm sure my men will be happy to donate from their civilian clothing."

A lump formed in her throat. He really was so sweet. "Thank you."

He gave her a rueful grin and shook his head. "I suspect that my crew will be more than anxious to give up their clothing for such a cause. I will have to limit it to no more than a few items per male or they will all be naked." He cleared his throat. "It would do me great honor if you would choose from amongst my clothing to create outfits for you and the girls."

His tail slipped over the arm she had curled around Tiana and gently stroked the baby's cheek.

Somehow she suspected that accepting his clothing was another act with more significance than she understood, but if it was important to him, she wasn't about to refuse him.

"It would be our honor," she said, echoing his words back to him.

Handing Tiana to him while she pulled her pants back on, she couldn't help but notice the way the baby watched him, her tiny tail seeking out his arm. Perhaps they did belong together, she thought, but just as the thought crossed her mind, Tiana's head started bobbing and didn't stop until her eyes found Abby. She stepped closer and put her hand on the baby's cheek, while Hrebec's other arm came around both of them. Even knowing that it was going to hurt that much worse in the end, she couldn't help but be glad that she would have the additional time with Tiana. And with Hrebec.

Pushing aside the sorrow of that future parting, she managed to smile up at him. "I think I'd better go rescue Pravit from Lucie. She's probably talked his ear off by now."

For a moment he looked startled, clasping a hand to

his almost nonexistent ear, then he smiled back. "I will assume that is another of your expressions."

"You would assume correctly. I'm going to get Lucie and then explain to the girls about the additional delay."

"I have duties as well." He rather reluctantly handed Tiana back to Abby, once again brushing his fingers against her breast in the process. Now that she knew how wonderful his hands felt on her body, it was even harder not to press against his hand. His breath caught as well, but he stepped back.

"If you do not object, I will join you for the mid-shift meal."

Her cheeks heated, but she nodded. "I would like that very much."

Pausing only long enough to drop a quick kiss on Tiana's head, and a slightly longer one on Abby's lips, he hurried away.

"That's your new daddy, Tiana," she said to the baby, who gurgled happily. "I just wish that didn't mean I can no longer be your mama."

With a heavy heart, she went to collect the daughter who would still be hers.

Mama and the Alien Warrior

Chapter Fourteen

To Abby's surprise, none of the girls seemed particularly upset about the additional delay.

TeShawna shrugged. "Ain't got nothing to hurry back to."

The other girls echoed the statement in their own ways. Of course. She should have considered that they'd ended up in her care originally because they had no one else to care for them.

Only Amber seemed to be concerned and pulled her to one side. "Miss Abby, what if I go into labor?"

"That's one of the reasons why I agreed to make this detour. This new planet has medical facilities."

"What if the baby doesn't want to wait?" She put a nervous hand on her stomach. "She's been awfully active."

Abby did her best to project a cool confidence that she did not feel. "Remember that the ship has a medical lab as well. Captain Hrebec has already explained things to the doctor so that he can prepare."

Fortunately, Amber hadn't seen Hrebec's distress when Abby had warned him, so she accepted the answer with a sigh of relief.

Molly, on the other hand, didn't even seem to think about her upcoming delivery. She was mooning around the cabin, staring at the door.

TeShawna came over to Abby and shook her head. "That girl's got it bad. She's tried to slip away twice, but I'm watching her."

"Thanks, TeShawna. I really appreciate that."

The girl just shook her head. "Don't reckon it'll do much good in the end. When they're that determined, they find a way. Least she can't get pregnant."

The rest of the day passed remarkably pleasantly. Lunch had been somewhat awkward, with the young crew members staring at the girls—and the babies—in silent awe. Not one of them had even so much as picked up a utensil until Hrebec growled at them. The girls were all flustered by the attention, but it was so obviously respectful that they eventually relaxed. TeShawna, with her usual bravado, even managed to wring a few words of conversation from one or two of the braver ones. Abby suspected it was just as well that Mekoi had not joined the lunch party.

Ensign Ribel had not joined them either, and after a despondent look around, Molly picked at her food. One of the other crewmen stuttered a few words to her, but she just shook her head and refused to look at him. Abby's concern for the girl continued to grow. Molly had been moody on Earth, but not to this extent.

After lunch, Hrebec escorted them to his ready room. He had provided more of the sealing wands, along with some cutting devices. The large conference table had been piled with garments, mainly white uniforms, but with an assortment of other colors sprinkled amongst them.

"Take your pick," he said to the girls, and then he handed Abby a large clear plastic box also packed with clothing. "These are for the three of you."

Aware that all of the girls were watching, she took the overflowing container and smiled up at him.

"I don't think we need this much."

"You deserve much more, but since this is all I can provide, I want you to take it all." He didn't kiss her, but his gaze felt like a caress as it traveled across her face before he bowed and left.

"Someone's got a crush on you," TeShawna teased.

"Oh, hush," she said, trying to hide her smile. "Now, who knows how to sew?"

As it turned out, Cassie had an extraordinary eye for fabric and cut. The high-tech tools delighted her and she immediately went to work. The rest of them simply followed her instructions.

"This is remarkable, Cassie," Abby said, holding up a tiny onesie made out of one of Hrebec's uniform shirts.

The girl shrugged. "When you've been dressed in hand-me-downs all your life, you learn how to adapt them. That wand thing makes it easy."

"This is more than adapting." Abby's eyes went to Lucie, who was happily skipping around the room in a cute little dress made from the rest of Hrebec's shirt. "You have a real talent for design."

Cassie scowled, uncomfortable with the praise, and for a moment, Abby thought she'd dismiss it entirely, but then her face softened. "I've always liked to sew. Even if it started out as a way to make an old piece of clothing my own." With a faint smile, she changed the subject. "No more cages and we get new clothes. This whole 'getting abducted by aliens' thing is looking up."

Abby surveyed the rest of the girls. Their laughter and conversation filled the room as they worked or juggled babies. Even Molly had roused from her usual moodiness to work diligently on a new outfit. If it weren't for the stars flowing past outside the window, they could have been back on Earth, gathered together in the big living room as they did most evenings.

"We're lucky the Cires found us," she agreed.

"Now what about you?" Cassie asked. "What are

you going to make?"

"I don't really need anything. I want to make sure Lucie and Tiana are taken care of first."

"They will be, but you can't keep wearing that ratty old sweater forever. Besides, I think that big captain would love nothing more than to see you in something made from his clothes." She pulled a garment that looked like a gold bathrobe out of the container. "Oh, this would be perfect with your complexion."

"Make it something sexy," TeShawna said, wandering over with her Vanessa in one arm and Cassie's Angel in the other.

Abby rolled her eyes, but the girls were right. A change of outfits probably wouldn't hurt.

Hrebec hurried back to his cabin, disappointed but not surprised that Abigail wasn't present. He was going to be unforgivably late for the evening meal. He took a quick shower and changed into a clean uniform, still fuming about the events of the afternoon. He had spent most of it with Mekoi, trying to prepare for the possibility that the pregnant females would give birth. Mekoi had sent a message to Ciresia, asking for copies of the older files that dealt with natural childbirth, and had been firmly refused. The High Council had no interest in assisting alien births and instead wanted the medic to run a series of tests on Tiana. Hrebec wasn't about to subject his new daughter to long-distance experiments, and he suspected that Abigail would be just as adamant.

Unable to receive assistance from his planet, he had reluctantly turned to the Vedeckian for aid. When Kwaret had been brought to the med lab, it was quite obvious that he had been abused by his fellow prisoners. One eye was swollen, his pale skin was bruised, and he walked with a slight limp. Furious, Hrebec questioned the very young guard who had been stationed outside the brig, only to find that he had actually heard sounds of struggle but decided it wasn't important since they were only prisoners.

"As long as I am in charge, no one on this ship will be mistreated," Hrebec snarled. "Do you understand me?"

"Yes, sir. I-I just thought—"

"You didn't think, Saprao. That is the problem. You will assist Pravit in the galley until we reach Trevelor."

"Yes, sir," Saprao said miserably. None of the crew liked assisting the crusty old warrior, and once Pravit knew he was being punished, Hrebec had no doubt that he'd make his life even more difficult.

"In addition, you will stay away from the human females. I do not trust you with their safety."

Saprao seemed to shrivel before his eyes, his face aghast as the consequences of his actions sank in, but Hrebec felt no sympathy. He had never expected that a member of his crew would be so lacking in compassion as to allow the abuse of a fellow being.

When he returned to the med lab, he reluctantly apologized to Kwaret. The man accepted it with a nervous smile, which did nothing to make Hrebec feel better. Fortunately, Kwaret possessed a surprising amount of knowledge about different methods of live birth. The three of them spent most of the afternoon making plans, and Hrebec came away with a begrudging respect for the Vedeckian.

When it came time to return Kwaret to the brig, he couldn't do it. Even though the guards were now alerted to the possibility of abuse and should be able to prevent any future violence, there was little they could do about verbal abuse. There were two small patient rooms attached to the lab. With Mekoi's permission, he decided to let Kwaret stay in one of them. However, Kwaret was still a Vedeckian and still a prisoner, so he would need to remain under guard. By the time Hrebec had completed the arrangements, he was late for dinner. Now he hastened down the corridor, eager to see Abigail and his girls again.

He entered the mess hall and stopped dead in his tracks.

No one had yet been seated. Instead, they lingered about in rather tentative groups. His eyes swept the room, dismissing everyone else, until he found his woman.

By Granthar, she froze him in his tracks.

Abigail wore a gown made from his clothing. He recognized the color and the material, but nothing else bore any resemblance to his mundane garment. Instead, the soft gold cloth draped down from one shoulder, leaving the other bare and revealing her delicate shoulder. The material gathered under her luscious breasts, then fell to her knees in a swirl of fabric. She looked beautiful, sensual, and tempting, and his cock strained against his pants even as his tail lashed, desperate to touch her. One of his ancestors would have had no hesitation in carrying her off and mating her, but, alas, these were more civilized times.

"Leonardo!" Lucie came dancing up, an enchanting sprite clothed in a dress made from one of his uniforms, and her presence distracted him from his lustful thoughts. "Look! I gots a new dress. Don't I look nice?"

"You look beautiful, little one," he said sincerely. When she smiled happily and held up her arms, he picked her up, her small body already a familiar weight against his shoulder. Abigail had followed her over, Tiana cradled in her arms, also in a new outfit, and the sight of all three of his females dressed in clothing that he had provided filled him with a sense of possessive pride. His tail caressed the infant's face and briefly circled Abigail's wrist before he wrestled it back under control.

"All of you look beautiful," he added. Abigail smiled at him, but worry shadowed her beautiful face. "Is there a problem, my flower?"

"Did you talk to your officer?" She nodded towards the viewport and his heart sank. Ribel was standing there, pointing out something to the young pregnant female. Ribel's tail circled her waist while she looked up at him with wide eyes, her face glowing.

"I'm afraid not. I apologize. There have been other matters requiring my attention, but that is no excuse for not keeping my word. I will talk to him as soon as the meal is over."

"Thank you." She gave him a rueful smile. "TeShawna thinks Molly will find a way to be with him no matter what we do, but she's just so young..."

"I will inform him. He'll do the honorable thing." *I hope.* "I am going to have him sit with me. Under the circumstances, perhaps it would be better if I didn't join you."

"I wants to sit with you, Leonardo," Lucie said, her eyes wide.

He gave Abigail a helpless look.

She shook her head, but smiled at him. "Is that all right with you?"

"Of course. I would have all three of you with me if I could." He suspected that his eyes betrayed his feelings, because Abigail blushed.

"Just please make sure she eats and doesn't spend all

of her time talking instead."

"I will retain my ear," he assured her.

She looked startled for a moment before her face lit up with a smile. "I am happy to hear that. I'm going to round up the girls and get everyone seated. Will you send Molly to me?"

"Of course." He bowed, then he and Lucie headed for the young couple.

His heart sank even more as he approached. He could tell by the scent that Molly's outfit had been created from Ribel's clothing. Aware that he had violated his own rule—he had forbidden his men to indicate who any of the donated items belonged to—he wondered how the girl had managed to find Ribel's garments.

"Ensign Ribel, you will join me for dinner." It was not a request, and he could see Ribel's mouth open to protest before he recollected himself.

"Yes, sir. Molly, will you—"

"Abigail is waiting for you," he said firmly to the young female.

She, too, looked as though she wanted to argue, but instead, she touched Ribel's tail briefly and went to join Abigail. Ribel opened his mouth again.

"I will talk to you after dinner," Hrebec said firmly. "In my office—no, my ready room."

"Yes, sir."

Lucie, obviously tired of being left out of the conversation, leaned forward and spoke to Ribel. "I gots a new dress."

To Hrebec's relief, the young officer tore his gaze away from Molly and spoke to Lucie. "I can see that. Did you make it?"

"I helped," she said proudly, then began instructing

them both on the art of dressmaking as he carried her to the table.

Mama and the Alien Warrior

Chapter Fifteen

The meal could not have been called a success. Although Hrebec enjoyed Lucie's company and her artless conversation, he wished Abigail had been next to him to enjoy it as well. Ribel spent most of the meal staring down the long table at Molly and tensing every time another crewman spoke to her. At least she ignored anyone paying attention to her and kept gazing at Ribel. Mekoi was not so lucky. TeShawna interacted with everyone in her vicinity, obviously enthralling the young crew members surrounding her, while his medical officer grew darker at each burst of laughter and his tail lashed angrily.

Jedan was the only one of his senior officers who enjoyed the meal. He had used the excuse of assisting Elaina with the second infant and had seated himself next to her. Watching the couple with the two babies made Hrebec's chest ache. He wanted that for himself—and he wanted it with Abigail. But he had promised to return her to her world and he would never break that vow.

As the meal wore on, he could also see the rising tension among his younger warriors as they all competed for the females' attention. There would be more training circuits in their future. Abigail, too, seemed aware of the rivalry, interjecting a soft word here or, if that didn't work, giving the man a stern glance. Fortunately, his crewmen responded well to her tactful censure. He would have hated to disturb the meal further by thrashing anyone who showed the slightest hint of disrespect to his woman.

Lucie was beginning to droop, her flow of conversation winding down and her small head resting more heavily against his side. He rose to his feet, cradling her against him. "I believe it is time to bring this meal to a conclusion. Ensign Ribel, your men will report to the training room. Jedan, if you would be so good as to escort the females to their quarters?"

"I will go as well," Mekoi said grimly. "To make sure that the infants do not need additional supplies."

Since he gazed at TeShawna as he spoke, Hrebec didn't believe that supplies were his primary concern, but he was willing to give his medic more leeway than he would his young crew members.

"Very well. Abigail, shall I carry Lucie to our—your cabin?"

"Yes, please," she said, giving him an unreadable look.

Together they waited until the others had left, then walked slowly back to his rooms.

"I was thinking," Abigail said, after she sent Lucie off to prepare for bed.

"Yes?"

"Would you like to stay here with us tonight?"

His heart started to pound, but he forced himself to remain calm. Her offer did not mean that she agreed to mate with him.

"I would be delighted, but why are you offering?"

She turned away from him, shifting Tiana to her shoulder and pacing as she rocked the infant. "If you're going to bond with Tiana, you should be here with her. It would help the transition."

Disappointment filled him. "I see."

She stopped, her back to him, and he could see her shoulders move as she took a deep breath before she turned to him. Her cheeks were his favorite shade of pink again.

"And I—I would like it as well." Pleased at her

admission, he took a step towards her and she raised a hand. "But we can't do anything that risks me getting pregnant."

"I understand." He didn't like it, but he understood her reasoning. However... "What about hankee pankee?"

Her blush intensified, deepening her pink to an enticing red. He knew that if she had a tail, it would be reaching for him.

She met his eyes directly. "I'm okay with that."

He bit back a groan. "I'm glad. I don't think I could share quarters with you and resist touching your sweet body."

She wet her lips and he made another move towards her, but then Lucie appeared in the bedroom door, dressed in a sleep garment made from another of his shirts. "I's ready."

"Okay, baby. I'll be right there."

"I want Leonardo to tell me a story."

"Not tonight," Abigail said firmly, before he could respond. "He needs to talk to someone first."

Lucie's bottom lip jutted out, but she looked at Abigail and didn't argue. Instead, she held up her arms to him. "Hugs and kisses," she demanded.

Without hesitation, he picked her up and hugged her gently as she kissed his cheek. The small gesture filled a piece of his soul that had been empty for far too long, and his chest ached with the realization of what he'd been missing. He carried her like precious cargo into the bedroom and reluctantly let her slide down under the covers.

"Will you be here tomorrow?" she asked.

"Yes, little one. I will be here." He had to fight the urge to promise her that he would always be there.

"Good," she said, giving him a sleepy smile.

Bending down, he kissed her forehead as his tail brushed along her tiny arm. He turned to find Abigail watching him again. She didn't comment, merely stepping aside to let him by.

"I'll be back shortly," he said.

"Good. We can see if Tiana will take her evening bottle from you."

"I look forward to it." He leaned forward and whispered in her ear, delighted when she shivered and her nipples tightened. "I also look forward to being alone with you."

"Me too," she whispered.

No longer reining in his instincts, he let his tail caress her beautifully pink cheek before walking away.

Hrebec left their cabin in a cheerful mood, one that only lasted until he reached the training room and found Ribel trying to kill Connep.

"What the hell are you trying to do?" he roared, as he forced his way between the two bruised and bleeding men.

Ribel continued to glare at Connep. "He tried to seduce my woman!"

"I was only talking to her," Connep protested as he sneered at Ribel. "But she is not your woman. She does not carry your scent."

Hrebec grabbed Ribel as the young man lunged forward.

"Listen, you young fools," he hissed. "She not only does not belong to either of you, but she is not a woman."

They both gaped at him.

"What do you mean?" Ribel asked. "Of course she is a woman."

"She is not of age in their society."

Ribel paled, and Connep stepped back.

"I don't understand. She is with child," Ribel said. "She must be old enough to mate."

"She is with child because someone took advantage of her innocence."

As comprehension slid over Ribel's face, it was rapidly replaced by rage. He turned and grabbed one of the massive weights they used in their training circuits, sending it flying across the room. It landed with a thunderous crash, immediately succeeded by four others. Hrebec didn't try and stop him; he understood the young man's rage.

The rest of the group looked equally appalled, although he suspected it was not as personal for them as it was for his ensign.

Connep turned to him and bowed his head. "Forgive me, Captain. I had no idea."

"I understand. You did not know—none of you knew." Looking up, he addressed the entire group. "But all of you must understand that these females are fragile. They were not treated well on their world. Fighting over them like a pack of *vultar* does nothing to make them feel safer in our presence. You must treat them with dignity and respect. Is that clear?"

A chorus of agreement filled the room, and looking around at their shamed faces, Hrebec thought that his message had been received. Ribel remained standing to one side, his head bowed and his tail lashing. Hrebec dismissed the rest of the crew and joined his young ensign.

"I am truly sorry, Ribel," he said. "I know this comes as a shock to you."

Ribel looked up at him, his face devastated. "But she's my mate. I'm sure of it."

"She is too young. I'm sorry." Hrebec sighed. "I wish you had not given her your clothing."

A puzzled look crossed Ribel's face. "I didn't give it to her. I was surprised—and delighted, of course—that she chose something of mine, but it was not of my doing."

Since Ribel had never been dishonest, Hrebec decided that the girl must have chosen his clothing by chance. Still, it was an unusual coincidence and he resolved to ask Abigail if there was some way the girl could have identified the garments.

They stood in silence for a few minutes before Ribel looked up at Hrebec. "But I was right, wasn't I? We can mate with them."

"I do not know if that is true," Hrebec said reluctantly.

Based on his encounters with Abigail so far, he had every expectation that they would be compatible and that he could knot inside her. Even the thought sent a rush of heat to his shaft, but at this point it was still conjecture. He had not verified their compatibility.

Ribel's face was a mask of amazement. "You mean that you and Miss Abby...?"

"That is not something I will ever discuss with you or anyone else."

"I'm sorry," Ribel said hastily. "It's just that the two of you appear to be a mated couple."

"The females are returning to Earth," he said, as much to remind himself as Ribel.

"I really thought... I hoped."

"I know. And perhaps you were right and I was wrong. Perhaps there are females out there who can save our race." The thought held no more than an abstract interest for him. Everything he wanted was upstairs in his cabin—

and he couldn't keep them.

He sighed and clapped Ribel on the shoulder. "Go on now. Make sure everyone understands what I said here tonight."

"Yes, sir." Ribel hesitated, wiping absently at the blood drying by his mouth. "And Molly?"

"I think it would be best for both of you if you stayed away from her, don't you?"

"I… I am willing to wait for her, no matter how long it would take."

For the impatient young officer, it was a surprising statement, but Hrebec saw only sincerity in his face.

"But she will not be here when she comes of age," Hrebec said gently.

"Could she stay with us? If she wanted to?"

Hrebec's thoughts went immediately to Abigail. Could she stay? Would she even choose to stay with him? No, it was a foolish thought.

"This is not their world," he reminded Ribel. "They were taken without their permission."

"From a world that did not appreciate them," Ribel responded.

Hrebec couldn't counter the argument. Instead, he shook his head. "They wish to return home."

Ribel looked at him for a long minute, before ultimately bowing his head. "Yes, sir."

He went on his way, his tail dropping. Hrebec shared his melancholy, but there was a bright spot to his circumstances. Abigail and his girls were waiting for him. It would be undignified for a captain to run, but he did set a rapid pace back to his cabin.

Mama and the Alien Warrior

Chapter Sixteen

Abby stared after Hrebec and hoped she wasn't making a mistake. When he'd made the remark about "their" cabin, she realized that a part of her had been expecting him to return tonight. Seeing him with Lucie just reinforced the expectation. And while it did make sense to encourage his bond with Tiana, a selfish part of her wanted him there for herself—to explore more of the delicious feelings he created. His touch reminded her that she wasn't just a mother; she was a woman too.

"Mama," Lucie demanded. "It's story time."

With a little laugh, Abby went back to motherhood.

Once Lucie was asleep, Abby showered, and after a brief hesitation, she changed into the nightgown Cassie had designed for her. Silky material crisscrossed her breasts before falling to a hem high on her thighs. True, she felt sexy, but also more vulnerable than she liked.

"This is ridiculous," she said to Tiana as she went to retrieve the familiar comfort of her cardigan.

Abby had converted Hrebec's storage container into a cozy bassinet and Tiana was lying in it, kicking her feet happily and blinking at her with big, dark eyes

"At least you're not nervous," Abby muttered as she reached for her sweater.

Before she could put it on, Hrebec appeared. The heat in his eyes—and his obvious physical response—erased most of her embarrassment.

"You are a vision, my flower," he said in a deep growl that set up an immediate ache between her legs.

"I'm glad you like it."

Tiana made a cooing noise and they both turned to her. She waved her arms and kicked her legs, her entire tiny body radiating with her delight.

"I think she's excited to see you," Abby laughed.

Hrebec went to the makeshift bassinet and carefully lifted her into his arms.

"You are a vision as well, little one," he said as her little sounds increased.

"That's the first time I've heard her respond like that," Abby said, trying for a cheerful voice, even though part of her was a little sad that the baby hadn't had the same response to her. "I doubt you'll have any problem feeding her."

Her optimism turned out to be misplaced. Tiana refused to take the bottle from Hrebec, whimpering and moving her head around until she found Abby.

"She wants you," he said with a sigh.

"But she's going to have to take food from you. How can I leave her if I don't know how she's going to eat?"

Hrebec looked at her, and she saw something in his face which made her breath catch in her throat, but all he said was, "Come closer."

Tiana calmed when Abby neared, but it wasn't until Abby actually touched her that she would take the bottle. Abby ended up sitting on Hrebec's lap while he cradled both of them and fed the baby. Tiana's eyes darted back and forth between their faces before she finally relaxed and began feeding with her usual enthusiasm. Hrebec wrapped his tail around them and Tiana's tiny one curled over it as she sucked.

"I like this," Hrebec said, his deep voice rumbling through her. "It's like we're a family."

She turned her head enough to see the wistful look on his face.

"It's just an illusion. Families don't last anyways," she said, but an unexpected longing softened her usual bitterness on the subject.

"Why would you say that?"

"Experience?" She shrugged, and the movement disturbed Tiana, who shot her a worried look. "Shh, sweetheart. It's okay." She stroked the baby's cheek and waited until she settled before she continued. "I suppose because my father left us when I was a young girl. He was bored with my mother. He did the same thing to his second wife after having a daughter with her, too."

"Your father left his mate? Left you?" Hrebec kept his voice low, but she could still hear his anger. "And left another child?"

"Yes. My half-sister, Lucinda. We didn't know about her for many years." She still remembered how shocked and excited she'd been to find out that she had a sister. Unfortunately, they had never developed a bond. She sighed. "I was lucky. My mother was a strong woman. She pulled herself together and worked hard to make sure I had everything I needed. Lucinda's mother fell apart after our father left and just drifted from man to man. I don't think they were nice men, and that's probably why Lucinda ran away. She didn't come to us and we couldn't find her either. Eventually, social services called me because they found Lucie."

Hrebec frowned. "Your sister took your child?"

"Oh, no. Lucinda gave birth to Lucie but she was involved with a very bad man, a drug dealer. I think she managed to stay off drugs while she was pregnant because Lucie is perfect, but as soon as she gave birth, she was back on them. She died from an overdose and I adopted Lucie."

"So she is not your daughter?"

"She is *absolutely* my daughter," she said indignantly.

"I did not mean to offend you. I just meant that you were not the one who birthed the child. Perhaps that is why you were able to bond with Tiana so easily—because you know that you don't have to give birth to be a mother."

"God, you understand that so easily. John couldn't seem to grasp it. He didn't understand why I didn't put her up for adoption, or at the very least hire a nanny to care for her."

"John?"

"My former partner. He only stuck around for a few months before he decided that having a baby around was too much trouble."

Hrebec growled. "I do not understand your Earth males. A child is a precious gift."

"They should be," she agreed. "But too many people are more interested in the pleasure of the act than the possible consequences."

"As I told you, a Cire isn't fertile unless he knots inside the female. And he will not knot unless he feels the possibility of a mating bond with her." His face was grave. "I feel that way for you, Abigail."

"I-I don't know what to say." She found the idea unexpectedly appealing, but it was impossible. *Wasn't it?* Yes, of course it was. She had a responsibility to her girls and she couldn't abandon them now. "I wish our circumstances were different."

He bowed his head but didn't speak.

In an attempt to change the subject, she brought up something she had noticed over the past few days. "Why is the majority of your crew so young?"

"It is... difficult to live on Ciresia. So many places were burned to the ground in a futile effort to contain the plague." His voice dropped. "Or because there was no other way to take care of those who died."

He gazed over her head, his eyes haunted, and Abby put a gentle hand on his arm as she waited for him to continue.

"Most of the remaining population has gathered in three smaller cities, each of them centered around a reproduction lab," he said at last. "I worked there for many years."

"You were a doctor?"

"No. I have some medical training, but I ran the lab. I monitored the projects, collated the data, made the reports. Year after year of failure." He shook his head again. "But you weren't asking about me."

"I want to know about you too."

"There isn't much to tell," he said bitterly. "No matter what I did, no matter what experts I recruited, what supplies I wrangled, what new experiments we tried, nothing helped. I spent most of my life there, following in my father's footsteps. When he died, I just couldn't do it anymore. The Confederated Planets are desperate for assistance. I commissioned a ship and was accepted into their volunteer fleet."

"Which leads us back to your crew," she prompted him.

He nodded gravely. "As I said, Ciresia is not a happy place. Even in the research cities, there are areas which have been burnt, abandoned. There is an overall air of... despair. For those few, like Ribel, who survived, they are young, energetic. They do not want to live out their lives in a mausoleum. When they found out I was leaving, they sought to accompany me and I could not turn them down."

"I'm surprised that a planet so desperate to repopulate would let them go."

He snorted. "There was a great deal of debate about it. In the end, I just took them and left."

"Does that mean you're in trouble with your government?"

He shrugged one massive shoulder. "They were not happy but they accepted it." He studied his hands. "Ironic, isn't it? Even the generation we created no longer wants to live on Ciresia. It's like a corpse that's still moving, not even aware that it's dead."

"You, um, don't look like an administrator," she said, trying not to stare at his impressive array of muscles.

"We were a warrior race. When I was young, the Red Death had not yet affected us to its full extent. I was trained as a warrior. The young men who survived were given the same opportunity."

What a complex man. She looked down at Tiana, cradled in one of those massive arms, and wondered what was going to happen to her. The baby had closed her eyes, even though her cheeks still moved, occasionally suckling.

"I think she's had enough. You need to burp her now."

She showed him how to burp the baby, then walked him through changing her bandage diaper and dressing her again. Tiana's eyes had closed again by the time he finished.

When Abby suggested he put Tiana in the bassinet, he frowned at the clear storage container. "I do not like this. It reminds me too much of the incubators. I would rather sleep with her on my chest."

"Are you going to bed now?" She raised an eyebrow.

"That was not my intention."

"Then put her down for now. You can get her again later."

"Very well."

He put the baby in the bassinet and carried it into the bedroom. Abby followed him to check on her other daughter. Lucie lay motionless on the bed, sleeping as deeply as always with one hand flung over her head and her body twisted sideways. Abby straightened her gently, checked the monitor bracelet, and then went to join Hrebec, closing the door behind her.

Mama and the Alien Warrior

Chapter Seventeen

Hrebec stood by his desk, pouring a glass of the strange liquor. "Would you like a drink?"

"No, thank you."

Tonight, she wanted to keep all of her wits about her. She suspected that it would be all too easy to succumb to her desire for Hrebec. Her pussy gave a responsive pulse at the thought of that massive nubbed cock sliding deep inside her empty sheath.

His head lifted and he turned to her. "You are aroused."

"How do you know?"

"Your scent. It is somehow sweeter."

Her cheeks heated but she didn't look away. Now that he had mentioned it, she noticed his as well. His usual lemony scent had taken on a deeper, almost musky note that seemed to heighten her own arousal. "You smell pretty good too. Does that mean you are aroused?"

"I am always aroused when you are around," he said, stepping towards her. This close, she had to tilt her head back to study his face, and the renewed awareness of his size and strength spurred her increasing desire. "But I'm surprised that you are aware of it as well. I thought that it was a Cire trait."

"Humans have a sense of smell too, you know."

Distracted by his closeness, she tugged at his shirt until it came free from his waistband. She slipped her fingers underneath, relishing all that warm, hard muscle and the intriguing texture of his jade skin. With an impatient growl, he yanked it off, giving her free access to his wonderful body.

"Yes, but scent bonding usually only occurs—" He broke off abruptly as she slid one of her hands around to his back and starting exploring his tail. "What are you doing?" "Touching your tail. Is that all right?" She couldn't get her hand around it, but she gave an experimental squeeze to the part she could reach.

He groaned. "Yes, that is most... pleasant."

"Pleasant? That's the best you can do? I must not be doing something right."

She stepped close, close enough that her arms could circle his narrow waist, close enough that her breasts pressed against his body. Now that both hands could reach, she used them to caress his tail in long, alternate strokes. His cock was a rock hard bar against her stomach and she could feel it jump with her movements, her nightgown growing damp with his precum. She lowered herself so that it could slide up between her breasts.

"Abigail!"

"Yes, Hrebec?"

"I am about to waste my seed."

"I don't consider it a waste."

She tightened her grip on his tail and used her arms to squeeze her breasts around his cock. His hands went to her back, holding her there as he began to thrust upward with his hips, the rapid movements fueling her own excitement. Her nipples were aching points, the texture of his skin an arousing massage as she rubbed against him. More moisture seeped from his cock, turning her nightgown translucent and letting her feel every inch of hard flesh as it moved between her breasts. She clamped down on his tail and let her nails dig in, just a little, but it was enough for him to give a low cry and erupt. His cock flexed against her as his seed shot forth, covering her upper body.

He had barely finished coming before he lifted her higher and started kissing her frantically, taking her mouth with a demanding urgency that left her dazed and clinging to him when he finally raised his head.

"I can't control myself around you," he said. He ran a finger down between her breasts to where his semen had soaked her gown and her skin. "This pleases me more than it should."

"I suspect that goes both ways." She shook her head as he carried her over to the couch. "I'm more attracted to you than I've ever been to another man."

He growled softly. "Do not talk to me of other men. May I remove this?"

"Might as well. It's kind of damp now. I guess I need to have Cassie help me make some other nightgowns."

"You do not need to conceal your beauty." He pulled the gown over her head, leaving her naked on his lap. She might have felt embarrassed if he weren't so obviously pleased. His fingers went back to her breasts, stroking the still damp skin. "I enjoy the scent of my seed on you."

The soft scrape of his fingers across the sensitive flesh made it difficult to concentrate on his words. "You mentioned scent bonding earlier. What does that mean? Is your sense of smell that strong?"

"I don't believe so, but—" His hand stilled. "There is a historical tale. A beautiful princess was sought by a warlord from a distant land. He sent his men to capture her and bring her to him. It was a long journey, and along the way, she fell in love with one of her guards. When she was brought before the warlord, she refused him and told him that her heart was already given. In his anger, he had her blinded. He then told her she could have her lover if she could identify him without sight or sound. He paraded his men before her, each one blindfolded and gagged. A hundred men went by, then a thousand, then finally, the princess cried out. She had found her lover. Without sight, without sound."

"By scent?"

"Yes."

"What happened to the princess and her lover?"

"The warlord let them go and they made their way back to the princess's land, where she eventually became queen and ruled for many years."

"I love that story." She smiled up at him. "Lucie would love it too. Except perhaps the princess should be blindfolded instead, just to be on the safe side."

His hand had stilled while he told the story, and she brought it over to cover her breast. He stroked a thumb across her nipple, but he still looked thoughtful.

"How did your females choose which garments to use to make their clothes today?"

"Really? *That's* what you're thinking about now?" A little annoyed, she started to pull away, but his hand tightened, sending a wave of pleasure straight to her aching pussy.

"Please, Abigail. This is important."

His dark eyes were intent on her face so she tried to think back. "Everything was stacked on the table, remember? The girls just went through them and picked out what they wanted."

"Did they smell them?"

"No—" A sudden memory made her hesitate. Molly had been reluctantly picking through the pile when she'd stopped and pulled out a shirt. Had she held it to her face? "Actually, I'm not sure. I think Molly might have. I know she held it up to her face." She sat up in his lap. "You aren't thinking of that story, are you? Molly is human, not Cire."

"And yet she chose something that had belonged to Ribel. He believes her to be his mate."

"Then he can *un*believe it. I told you she's too young."

"I relayed that to him," he said soothingly, but then he frowned. "He said he was willing to wait, no matter how long it took for her to come of age."

"He's young. He'll get over it. They both will." She tried for a dismissive tone, despite her own concerns about Molly.

"Perhaps. Did you know that we rescued another group of females previously?"

"Oh?" A distinct pang of jealousy hit her. Had Hrebec been involved with one of them?

"Yes. They were Villae. Tiny little things. Quite beautiful." He must have felt her instinctive withdrawal, because he pulled her closer and gave her a quick kiss. "Of course, none of them were as beautiful as you. My point was that Ribel was fascinated by them, but they were all the same to him. He never fixated on one the way he has with Molly. And he would never have waited for one."

"But she's going back to Earth."

"And he will have lost his mate."

She wondered if the desolation in his voice was entirely about his ensign. There was an ache in her own heart that she preferred not to think about.

Forcing a smile to her lips, she reached up and ran her fingers along that strong jaw. "Maybe we should stop worrying about them. At least for tonight."

He almost visibly pushed away his concerns and smiled down at her. "I am a fool. I have a beautiful female in my arms—I should be paying attention to her."

"Yes, you should." She reached down and stroked the nub-covered tail that had curved around her waist. "Should we try some more forbidden things?"

A very long, pleasurable time later, Hrebec carried his sleeping woman to bed. He had made her climax twice, first with his tongue and then with his tail, before he allowed himself to succumb to her wicked hands and spill his seed onto the pale curve of her stomach. Their scents mingled in a heady mix that had his cock in a state of constant aching hardness. He suspected it would remain that way unless he ever had the ecstasy of being inside her.

As he went to put her down, her eyes fluttered open. "I need to put some clothes on."

"Why? You look most delightful this way."

"Thank you. But I need to be prepared in case one of the girls wakes up and needs me."

"Very well. Stay here."

He left her on the bed and went to his locker, pulling out an old shirt, soft with age. She looked at it, then at him, finally shaking her head and raising her arms so he could drop it over her head. As expected, it was much too large for her small body, but he still felt an immense satisfaction at seeing her in his clothing.

"You really like seeing me in your clothes, don't you?" she said with a smile and a quick stroke of his once again aching erection. Before he could respond, she removed her hand. "Now you put something on too. Just in case."

By the time he returned, her eyes were closed. He pulled Lucie's feet away from Abigail's stomach, then took Tiana out of the horrible container and placed her on his chest. She blinked drowsy dark eyes at him and went back to sleep. Gazing at her, he turned over the events of the day in his head until he finally decided on a course of action. Satisfied, he went happily to sleep.

Unfortunately, he did not remain asleep for long. The sound of Lucie moaning penetrated his slumber.

"Mama, I don't feel good," she said pitifully, just before she spewed a foul liquid over half the bed.

He managed to keep Tiana out of the way, but his side and pants were soaked.

"What's wrong?" he asked Abigail frantically. "Shall I send for Mekoi?"

He was halfway to the message panel before the calm reasonableness of her voice stopped him. "Just wait a minute. What's the matter, baby?"

"My tummy hurts," Lucie said, sounding close to tears.

His heart pounded. "The medic—"

"Calm down, Hrebec. What did she eat for dinner?"

"For dinner?" He tried to force aside his alarm and concentrate. "Just *flodan* pastries."

"And?"

"That was all. She said she liked them the best."

"You let her eat nothing but sweets?" Abigail rolled her eyes. "No wonder she threw up. I should make you clean all of this up."

"Of course I will. But that is why she is ill? Because of me?" Shame and horror filled him. How could he have failed at his responsibilities so badly? He looked down at Tiana, sleeping so trustingly in his arms. Would he fail her as well? "I am unfit to be a father."

"It's just a rookie mistake—a new parent mistake." Abigail began stripping away Lucie's night garments, her face serene. Did she really not blame him? "Why don't you put Tiana in the bassinet and go grab some clean bedding? I'm going to pop Lucie in the shower."

He gave the little girl a worried look, but she was already looking better. While Abigail bathed Lucie, he hurried to obey her request, remaking the bed with clean, sweet smelling linens. He then washed at the small sink in his office and changed his own clothing. When they returned, Lucie bounced up to him, her usual humor restored.

"S'okay, Leonardo. Mama said I shouldn't a let you give me all the good stuff." She made a face. "I has to eat vegetables and yucky stuff so I can grow up big and strong."

Her words didn't help. "I stunted your growth?"

Abigail gave him a soft smile. "Hrebec, it was only one meal. She's fine."

"Mama says all the bad stuff is gone now," Lucie said cheerfully.

"I'm very glad." His knees were weak with relief.

"Me too. I don't like feeling yucky." Lucie sighed. "No more sweet stuff."

Her little face was so woebegone that, even in spite of the evening's events, he wanted to promise her she could have whatever she wanted. Fortunately, Abigail intervened.

"I said you could have dessert—*after* you ate your vegetables. Now back to bed, you little minx."

Lucie jumped up on the bed and gave him a pleading look. "I's awake now. Tell me a story."

He looked at Abigail, and she nodded. He sat down on the bed and Lucie snuggled against him. While he told her the story of the princess, Abigail moved quietly around the room, tidying up as she went. Lucie fell asleep before he finished the tale.

"Are you certain that Mekoi doesn't need to see her?"

he asked as Abigail returned to bed.

"It was just an upset stomach. You saw for yourself how quickly she recovered. Children are very resilient."

"That was not been my experience."

"I know, Hrebec, and I'm very sorry." She carefully moved Lucie to one side so she could curl up next to him instead.

As she ran a soothing hand down his chest, his body immediately started to respond, but his worries still consumed him. "How am I going to take care of Tiana?"

"You'll learn. Every parent has to do it." She yawned and snuggled closer. "As long as you love her, it will be fine."

A few minutes later, she was asleep. He gently disengaged her long enough to bring Tiana back to bed with them. The infant's eyes opened, dark and serious in the quiet room.

"I will take care of you," he vowed.

A toothless grin dissolved into a yawn as her tail came up and circled his wrist

His chest ached. "I love you, little one."

Lucie made a soft noise in her sleep and his tail automatically moved to pat her shoulder while Abigail settled more fully against him.

"I love all of you," he whispered, studying his sleeping girls. "And I'm going to lose you."

Mama and the Alien Warrior

Chapter Eighteen

T he next morning, Abby insisted that Hrebec try feeding Tiana again. He eventually succeeded, although not without Abby touching the baby. Even then, she didn't feed well and her tail gripped Abby's wrist the entire time. She tried not to let it worry her—it was only the second time he'd tried—but she felt an underlying sense of panic. Hrebec looked equally as worried.

"Why don't you take her with you today?" she suggested. "You can still bring her back for feeding times," she added hastily. "But this will give her a chance to spend time with you."

"I cannot carry her the entire time."

"You could take her bassinet." When he cast it a look of acute dislike, she said, "Or we could rig up a snuggy?"

"A what?"

"A sort of sling. To carry her against your chest."

"That would be acceptable."

Together they managed to wind a length of material around his chest and form a pouch for the baby. He should have looked ridiculous, but the sight of the big warrior with the tiny baby tucked to his chest made her heart—and other parts—warm. From the heated look in his dark eyes, she suspected that he had detected her arousal. He took a step towards her, but Lucie interrupted.

She pointed at the sling. "I wants Leonardo to carry me that way."

To Abby's surprise, he answered perfectly. "But you're a big girl now. Big girls ride differently."

Abby choked and turned away, cursing her dirty mind.

"Perhaps after the mid-shift meal, you can spend some time with me?" He glanced at Abby. "If your mother approves."

Lucie was already bouncing up and down. "She will, won't you, Mama?"

Two sets of dark eyes looked at her, one human brown and the other reptilian black, but their pleading expressions were identical.

"Fine," she laughed. "Tiana can come and take a nap with me."

Hrebec left with Tiana, but not before giving Abby a kiss, just long enough to arouse her interest.

Lucie giggled. "Leonardo's kissing Mama."

She then proceeded to repeat her observation to the girls when they gathered for breakfast in the ready room. They had agreed to meet there since, as TeShawna put it, "They didn't need no man staring at them before they had their coffee."

While they didn't actually have coffee in space, there was a pale beverage with a slightly salty taste that had the same effect. Abby almost choked on hers when Lucie repeated her earlier comment.

"Nice that someone's getting some," TeShawna muttered.

Abby gave her a worried look. The girl looked tired and annoyed, her usual good-natured bravado absent.

"She had a fight with that doctor last night," Cassie murmured quietly, but TeShawna overheard.

"Damn right I did. I don't need another jealous asshole in my life. 'Specially when most of 'em have a girl in every port and a wife at home anyway."

"Damn right, damn right," Lucie sang.

"Lucie, those are big girl words," Abby told her.

"You mustn't repeat them."

Her little chest puffed out. "Leonardo says I'm a big girl."

"You're not *that* big yet," she said firmly. "Now, why don't you go with Miss Cassie and let her make you some new pants?"

"I don't want pants. I wants a dress."

"Come on, little bit. I bet there's enough material for both." Cassie drew Lucie to the other end of the room.

"It's not like that with these men, TeShawna," Abby said quietly. "Their women died."

"What?" A look of unwilling sympathy crossed TeShawna's face. "You mean he lost his wife?"

"No. I don't think he was ever married. There was an illness and they lost all of their women. As far as they know, Tiana is the only one."

"Is that why they're giving us the bum's rush?" TeShawna's words may have been cynical, but Abby saw the sadness in her eyes.

"Poor Jedan." Elaina's eyes filled with tears. "He's so good with Ginger. He'd make a wonderful daddy." She smiled ruefully, and Abby noticed that she, too, looked pale and tired. "I coulda used his help last night. Two babies are a lot to handle."

"*Two*? Molly didn't help you?" Abby looked around and saw the girl slumped against the back wall, staring out at the stars.

Elaina shrugged her shoulders. "I went to find her, but she was gone."

"Damn. She must have snuck out while I was putting that ass—doctor in his place." TeShawna sounded more sad than angry.

"She wasn't gone that long," Amber volunteered. "I

tried to tell her that Elaina needed some help, but she wouldn't even look at me. Just crawled into bed and put her face to the wall."

Abby hoped that meant that Ribel had told the girl that there was no future between them, but looking at her, her heart still ached for the young girl's obvious pain.

"Just like Romeo and Juliet," Amber sighed.

TeShawna clicked her teeth in disgust, but a new worry intruded into Abby's thoughts. Surely the girl wasn't so far gone that she would try and kill herself? Looking at the despondent little figure, she couldn't entirely be sure.

Biting her lip, she turned back to the other girls. "Let's have breakfast. Then we can do some more sewing."

The morning continued quietly enough and Abby eventually managed to coax Molly into eating a few bites.

"Is there anything you want to talk about, Molly?" she asked, but the girl glared at her with furious resentment.

Abby suspected that Ribel had told her why he wasn't going to see her again. She sighed, deciding to drop it for the time being. It was best to give Molly a chance to cool off before she tried to press the issue again.

Turning to Lucie instead, she made sure that her daughter had fruit and some kind of cereal-like dish for breakfast instead of more pastries. After the meal, they resumed their sewing. It wasn't until she saw Elaina pick up a shirt, wrinkle her nose, and put it back down that she thought about the previous night's conversation.

"Elaina, was there something wrong with that shirt?"

"Nah. It just didn't seem right."

The girl shrugged, but a few minutes later, Abby saw her pick up another identical shirt. This time, she smiled and kept it. Curious, Abby picked up one of the garments from the communal pile. Even before she raised it to her face, she knew she didn't like it. There was nothing specific, just an overall feeling of rejection.

As the morning passed, she realized that TeShawna had the same reaction, going through several shirts before she picked one. Abby was willing to bet it belonged to Mekoi. Neither Amber nor Cassie seemed bothered by any of the garments, but Molly picked one up and immediately discarded it. She picked up a second one, then hugged it close as she started to cry.

Abby went to her and put her arms around the girl. For a moment she stiffened, then she gave in and sobbed against Abby's shoulder.

"He thinks I'm too young," she said finally. Her look was worse this time, filled with betrayal rather than anger.

"You *are* young, Molly," Abby said gently.

"But I'm not a child." Her hand went to her stomach as she snorted a bitter laugh. "Doesn't this prove that?"

"You don't have to be grown up to get pregnant, honey," Elaina said.

"But I've never felt like this before!" Molly wiped her eyes and sat up. Abby wished she had a dollar for every girl that had said the same thing, but there was an earnestness to Molly's speech that she couldn't ignore. "Before, with Bill, I always felt small and helpless, and he made me feel safe. But with Ribel—he still makes me feel safe, but I also feel stronger. Like I'm better when he's around."

"Ain't you forgetting he's an alien?" TeShawna broke in. "Doesn't matter how he makes you feel. We're going back to Earth, and he can't come."

The blunt words cast a pall over the rest of the morning. Abby was conscious of the same feeling of depression, no matter how ridiculous she told herself she was being. TeShawna was perfectly correct. The Cires were aliens and they were humans. *There's no future here,* she told herself.

Her words rang hollow, especially when lunch rolled around and once again, she helped Hrebec feed Tiana. Despite their differences, they felt like a family—a feeling that was only reinforced when he took Lucie for the afternoon, swinging her up on his shoulder for her "big girl" ride. She squealed with delight and clutched his head.

"Bring her back to our—your cabin in a few hours. I want to talk to you."

He nodded gravely, then shrugged his shoulder to bounce Lucie and making her squeal again. As they turned to walk away, Abby saw that his tail and his hand were holding her daughter firmly in place. A warm glow filled her. Hrebec would never let her fall.

"Where do you want to go, Princess Lucie?" Hrebec asked as they left the dining hall.

"Where does you drive the ship?"

"It's called the bridge. I'll take you there."

When he walked on to the expansive bridge, there was a startled silence for the second time that day. His men had been more than a little surprised when he'd appeared with Tiana earlier, although that hadn't stopped them from gathering around to admire her. The infant looked at them with her wide-eyed gaze. She didn't seem afraid, but her tiny fist remained clenched in his shirt and her tail wrapped around him every time he adjusted her position.

"A Cire female," Maraq breathed. "I never thought to see one."

Hrebec remembered that Maraq had been on duty the previous day and had missed the joint meals, but he found himself surprisingly annoyed. "She is my daughter. She is not an object of curiosity."

"Yes, Captain. I didn't mean it that way." Maraq hesitated, then said cautiously, "Your daughter?"

"Unless we find that she has living family on Trevelor." Even the thought made his chest ache. He couldn't bear to lose not only Abigail and Lucie but Tiana as well. Pushing the unwelcome possibility aside, he frowned at his men. "Don't you have work to do?"

The morning had proceeded as normal after that. Despite more than a few glances in her direction, Tiana had been so quiet that it had been easy for his men to maintain their routine.

He suspected Lucie would be another matter—a suspicion that was confirmed as soon as they walked on to the bridge.

"Hi!" she called cheerfully, and loudly. "I'm Princess Lucie, and Leonardo is my horsie!"

Inzen came up and bowed to her. He was the chief engineer, and another senior member of the crew. "How do you do, Princess Lucie?"

She beamed at him and waved an imperious little hand. "I'm just fine, thanks." Her attention was drawn to the huge screens that lined the front of the bridge. "What's those? Are they TVs?"

"They are screens that let us see where we are," Inzen said. "I think I know something you would like to see." He went to his desk and worked at his controls for a few seconds before the screens lit up, showing an array of planets with a brilliant pink nebula shining beyond them.

"It's so pretty," Lucie gasped, then relapsed into silence, her arm clutching his head as she stared and stared. Hrebec stood there, letting her take in the sight, seeing the magnificent display as if for the first time through her eyes. Eventually, she wiggled. "Does you have Frozen?"

"Frozen?"

"The movie? With Queen Elsa and the ice palace?"

He wasn't entirely sure what she was asking for, but it sounded like entertainment of some kind. "I'm afraid not, little one."

"You can't see any other shows?"

"No."

"This is a good one," she said. "But I like singing ones too."

He had the most ridiculous urge to sing for her. Instead, he lowered her down to chest level. "Would you like to see what we do here?"

"Okay," she agreed, her sweet smile lighting her face.

He hugged her, his tail curled around her back, before taking her from station to station and introducing her to the rest of the bridge crew. When she got bored with that, Inzen handed her a tablet and showed her how to play a simple game.

When Lucie became engrossed in her game, Hrebec settled her into his chair before strolling over to Inzen. "I wasn't aware that Reserve tablets were equipped with children's games."

Inzen's cheeks darkened, but he shrugged. "I just wrote a little program. If she likes it, I can make more."

Hrebec clasped his shoulder. "Thank you, my friend."

"There is no need for thanks." Inzen's eyes went to Lucie. "It does my old heart good to see a child again, especially such a happy one. I will pray to Granthar that she is always this content."

"As will I," Hrebec said, following his gaze. For as

long as she was with him, he would do everything in his power to ensure her happiness.

Mama and the Alien Warrior

Chapter Nineteen

Lucie pouted when Hrebec said it was time to return to their cabin, but Inzen consoled her when he assured her that she could keep the tablet. Instead of returning to her seat on Hrebec's shoulders, she ran ahead of him, her voice echoing through the corridors as she skipped along singing an incomprehensible song about letting go. As soon as they reached the cabin, she rushed inside.

"Mama! Leonardo's got TV but he only gots a pink show, not Frozen. And I's got a present."

"You do? What is it?" Abigail smiled at her daughter from where she was sitting on the couch, sorting through a pile of clothing.

"It's a game! Inzen gave it to me. I like him a lot! But 'course, not as much as Leonardo."

"Of course not," she agreed solemnly.

"Do you like him best too, Mama?"

"Yes, sweetie. I do." She looked directly at him as she spoke, and joy coursed through him.

"Do you likes us best too?" Lucie asked him.

"Yes, I do," he assured her.

"Good," she said, around an enormous yawn.

"Time for a nap, sweetie."

"I's not sleepy, Mama."

"You can still go lie down," Abigail said firmly. "And you have to be quiet. Tiana's asleep."

With a defeated sigh, Lucie turned to him. "Carry me, Leonardo."

He obeyed, carrying her into the bedroom and laying her down in the center of his big bed.

Before he could stand up, her tiny arms closed

around his neck and she kissed his cheek. "I love you, Leonardo."

His throat tightened to the point where it was difficult to speak, and his words came out in a hoarse whisper as his tail tenderly touched her cheek. "I love you too, little one. Now close your eyes and rest."

"Okay," she said, smiling up at him.

As he turned to leave the room, he glanced at Tiana and realized that Abigail had done something to the container. The walls were no longer clear but had fabric fastened to the outside with tiny bows. The delicate touches made it appear more comfortable, like home, and less like the dreadful incubators. His chest ached. Abigail had done that for him.

When he returned to the front room, Abigail was still sitting on the couch. He swept her up and settled down in her place with her on his lap, kissing her until she was breathless.

She stared up at him, her pale eyes dazed. "What in the world was that for?"

"For covering the container."

"The container? Oh, you mean the bassinet." Her cheeks turned that lovely shade of pink. "I saw how much you disliked it, but you can't carry her all the time."

"It is a vast improvement, and I thank you."

"I'm afraid she'll outgrow it soon. We—you will need to find another place for her to sleep. Do you still have baby stores on Ciresia?"

"No," he said shortly. Perhaps there were some that had not yet decayed, but he would not use anything from one of those sad reminders of the past for his sweet daughter.

"No, I suppose not." She bit her lip. "Maybe when

you take us back to Earth, you could stay for a little while? I could get her some supplies there."

He wanted to—oh, how he wanted to—but he knew he could not. "Confederated Planets law forbids contact with developing worlds. We will use the shuttle to transport you at night, but it would be too risky to stay any longer than absolutely necessary."

"I suppose you're right." She didn't sound any happier about it than he felt.

He attempted to distract her. "What are you doing with those garments?"

A number of uniform shirts had been folded into neat piles.

She pursed her lips. "I know these aren't labeled, but can you tell who they belong to?"

He reached for one, then nodded. "Yes."

"By scent? Even though they're clean?"

"Yes, of course. Once an object has been worn, it picks up an... essence of the wearer that is not removed, even by washing. These all appear to have been worn."

"Can you line them up on the desk? So that they're as identical as possible?"

"Of course."

He reluctantly put her aside, missing the feel of her body as soon as he did so. When he stood up, she closed her eyes. It wasn't until he noticed that one of the shirts was his that he realized what she was doing. His heart began to pound as he set the folded uniforms in a neat row on his desk.

"They're ready," he said.

She opened her eyes and came over to join him. One by one, she picked up the shirts and lifted them all to her face, despite her obvious reluctance as they came close to her. Her face crinkled with each shirt, until she came to his and she finally relaxed as she held it closer.

"This is yours, isn't it?"

"Yes, my flower." His heart was singing but she looked too troubled for him to rejoice. "Does that worry you?"

"I'm not sure I understand what it means."

It means that you are my mate. But he didn't say the words aloud.

"TeShawna and Elaina are reacting the same way," she said finally. "And Molly."

"That is... unexpected," he said slowly. "It was clear that there was an attraction, but they are acting more like Cire females."

He didn't mention that she was reacting the same way, but the knowledge hung in the air between them.

"This repulsion to another man's smell—that's normal?"

"Yes."

"Do you—do Cire males react the same way?"

"Yes." He looked directly at her. "I would know your scent anywhere, Abigail. No other would appeal to me."

She bit her lip and gave a nervous little laugh. "But you'll get over that, right? Once we're apart?"

No. He strongly suspected that no other female would ever appeal to him. But he couldn't tell her that. He didn't want her to feel sorry for him, or for her to feel that he was trying to force her to stay with him. Instead, he shrugged and changed the subject.

"Do you require anything else for your females?"

"No." She gave him a warm smile. "You have provided for us very well. Did you talk to Dr. Mekoi about the possibility that one of the girls might give birth?"

"Yes, and he is making preparations." He added reluctantly, "Kwaret had been assisting him."

"See? They're not all bad."

"No. I suppose all races have both good and bad members. Unfortunately, the Vedeckian culture places profit above all else. He is the only one I have met who seems to have some respect for other values."

"After the girls wake up, I'll go and see if I can provide any help. I might not have any personal experience but I've been through a number of births with my girls."

He did not like the idea of her in the same room with the Vedeckian male—or with any male for that matter—if he could not be present, but he understood her sense of responsibility. "Is that your employment?"

"More of a labor of love, really. After I adopted Lucie, I didn't want to leave her with a nanny all day. I was a chief financial officer for a large corporation and they thought that children should come second to the responsibilities of my job. I disagreed. So I resigned and decided to open a maternity home for pregnant girls with nowhere else to go." She looked away from him. "That was another reason that John left. He wanted a partner with an impressive title, not to mention an income that allowed her to purchase the appropriate clothing." Running a thoughtful hand over her mended pants, she shook her head. "He certainly wouldn't have approved of clothing made from someone else's leftovers."

"I like this male less and less each time you mention him," he growled.

"I did too." She shrugged. "He was fine when everything was easy, but he wasn't about to make any sacrifices to support my needs, let alone Lucie's. I wasn't even surprised, really. Most men are like that."

"No, they are not. A true male would make any sacrifice for his mate. I—" *I would do anything for you.*

"You?" she asked, her head tilted and her eyes glimmering with what looked like hope.

"I—I have duties to attend to. I will join you for the evening meal."

He was a coward, and yet how could he tell her how he felt when she planned to leave him? Still, he lingered long enough to kiss her, hoping to convey with his body what he could not say with his words. She melted against him, her soft body arousing his desire. When at last he strode away from their cabin, the ache in his loins matched the ache in his heart.

Under the circumstances, he was not surprised when Jedan sought him out just before dinner. Since he was sharing his cabin with Abigail and the females had taken over his ready room, he was using a former supply room as a small office and Jedan found him there.

"Captain Hrebec." Jedan stood at attention, his gaze fixed on the wall.

"Yes, Lieutenant?"

"I wish to inform you that I have moved Elaina and the two infants into my quarters."

Hrebec closed his eyes. He should have known that this was coming. "It didn't occur to you to ask my permission?"

"No, sir." Jedan's eyes flashed to his for the merest second. "I was merely following the precedent which you set."

That was also something he should have expected. "I

assume she is willing?"

"Of course she is!" Jedan finally dropped his formality. "It is very difficult for her to look after both infants on her own. I wish only to assist her."

"That is your only wish?" Hrebec asked dryly.

"No." His second hesitated, then sighed and sat down. "I wish to take her as my mate, to care for her and the infants for the rest of their lives. But I know she is returning to their planet and that I will not be able to accompany her. She has told me that her people would react with fear. That alone would not bother me, but she says that her government would take me away from them."

"If it were not for that, you would go? Knowing that you would never see Ciresia again?"

Sorrow cast a shadow on Jedan's face. "You know as well as I do that Ciresia was lost to us many years ago. I would miss this ship and her crew, of course, but Elaina and the children are more important to me. I would give up everything to keep them."

"I know, Jedan." Hrebec couldn't argue, because he would do the same given the opportunity. "I know."

Mama and the Alien Warrior

Chapter Twenty

After Hrebec left, Abby gathered the extra uniform shirts to return to the ready room and started working on a surprise for Lucie. They had taken some of Hrebec's uniform fabric and boiled it with some dried fruit that Pravit had provided, turning the fabric a soft pink. As soon as she heard Lucie stirring, she hid the partially completed dress under some other clothing.

Lucie appeared in the bedroom door, rubbing her eyes and yawning. "Tiana's awake, Mama."

"Thank you, baby."

While Abby fed and changed Tiana, Lucie wandered around the small room. As she traced the carving on Hrebec's desk, she came to the pile of uniform shirts and wrinkled her nose.

"Why does you have these smelly shirts, Mama?"

"Why *do* I," she corrected automatically before she realized what Lucie had said. "Wait, smelly? Do they all smell bad?"

Lucie picked through them, grabbing one with a smile on her face. "Not this one. I likes this one."

Oh, good lord, it was affecting all of them. *All of them...*

She looked down at Tiana who nursed contentedly. "Lucie, baby, can you bring me one of those shirts that smells good and one that smells bad?"

Lucie made a face but obeyed. "Here you go."

Abby took the first one, one that didn't belong to Hrebec, and brought it closer to the baby. Her little face wrinkled and she stopped sucking.

"Sorry, sweetie," Abby said, hastily removing the

offending garment.

Once Tiana started working away at her bottle again, she draped Hrebec's shirt over her arm. Tiana didn't stop nursing but she definitely slowed down and her tail clung more tightly to Abby's arm.

"What's you doing?"

"I was trying to see if Tiana thought the shirts smelled bad. Since she's just a baby, she can't tell us."

"I know. I have lots to teach her," Lucie said importantly. "When's she going to be big enough to play with me?"

"Not until after we go home, I'm afraid."

"I don't wants to go home. I wants to wait until Tiana can play with me." Lucie pouted and her eyes shimmered with unshed tears.

Seeing Lucie so upset had Abby's own heart aching.

"I know you do, sweetie." *So do I.* "As soon as Tiana's done, why don't we go show Cassie your new game? I need to go talk to the doctor again."

"I 'spose," Lucie said reluctantly.

Lucie kept pouting until they reached the girls' quarters, where she forgot her troubles in her excited rush to show Cassie her new toy. Cassie was suitably admiring, but once Lucie was engrossed in another game, she came over to Abby.

"Do you think they could make a formula for Angel the way they did for Tiana?"

"I don't see why not. They seemed to understand what a baby needs from a nutritional viewpoint. If it's not being served cold from a tube, you could probably get her to take it. And I'm sure Dr. Mekoi would be willing to help us find the right combination."

"What's the matter?" TeShawna huffed. "My milk

not good enough?"

"Oh, TeShawna, you know better." Cassie's eyes filled with tears. "You saved her life and I can never forget that. But I miss feeding her. At least with a bottle, I could still do that."

"Yeah, I guess I can understand that." TeShawna's face softened, but Abby couldn't help noticing that she still looked tired and drawn.

"I need to talk to the doctor anyway," Abby said. "Why don't you come with me, TeShawna? You can tell Dr. Mekoi about Angel's eating habits." She hoped it wasn't a mistake to bring her along, but she couldn't stand seeing her so miserable.

"I reckon I could."

Cassie winked at Abby. "I'll take care of the girls."

All of the cabin doors were open. Abby could see Molly lying on her bed, staring at nothing, while Amber was walking Lily around, singing to her.

"Where's Elaina?"

"She moved in with that Lieutenant Jedan," TeShawna muttered, not even bothering to mask her resentment.

"She did what?" *Oh, crap.* Although after her little experiment with the shirts, why was she even surprised?

"Seems like she's following in your footsteps," the girl added.

"But that's different," Abby protested weakly. "Hrebec is just helping me with the girls."

TeShawna raised her eyebrows. "And Jedan is just helping her with Mikie and Ginger. Alone. In his cabin."

As TeShawna's words sank in, Abby swore under her breath. Considering how hard it was for her to keep her hands off of Hrebec, could she expect Elaina to have the same restraint?

Abby sighed. "I definitely need to go see Mekoi now. Are you coming?"

"I said I would."

Despite her apparent reluctance, TeShawna led the way down the corridor to the med lab. Abby watched as she stepped into the room. Even though anger still darkened her face, her body relaxed as soon as she entered.

"TeShawna. I am very glad to see you," Mekoi said gravely as his tail flicked towards her. "You did not give me an opportunity to finish—"

"I heard enough," she muttered. "I'm not here to see you, anyways. Miss Abby wants to talk to you."

Mekoi bowed his head and his tail drooped. "I see."

Abby decided that the time had come to intervene. "Hrebec told me that you're making preparations in case one of the girls goes into labor before we reach Trevelor."

"That is correct." He gestured to an open door on the far side of the room. Inside, she saw Kwaret working on some type of machine. "Kwaret has been most helpful."

TeShawna wandered over to the room and raised her eyebrows. "You've got enough equipment in here to choke a horse. My granny gave birth with nothing but a pot of hot water and some string."

"Water? Why do we need water? Or string? Those were not on our list." Mekoi's face assumed a panicked expression.

"The hot water was to sterilize everything, and the string was used to tie off the umbilical cord," Abby explained. "And TeShawna, you know that there was a lot of equipment at the hospital."

"Just saying." She shrugged.

"Everything will be sterilized," Mekoi assured them

both. "And we have clamps to separate the umbilical cord. I just wish I knew more about the process."

"Then it's a good thing I brought TeShawna along. She can describe the procedure when she gave birth," Abby said cheerfully. "Why don't you see what they have set up, TeShawna?"

The girl made another face but disappeared into the room, and a moment later, she could be seen questioning Kwaret intently. Mekoi went to join them, but Abby stopped him.

"Dr. Mekoi, are you familiar with birth control? To prevent pregnancy?"

"Of course I am familiar with the concept." A shadow crossed his face. "It has been forbidden on Ciresia since the third year of the Red Death."

"I can understand that, but now we have humans and Cires in, um, close companionship. I wouldn't want any unexpected consequences."

"You mean that humans and Cires can mate?" he asked eagerly. "But this is wonderful news."

"I don't know if they can or not," she said quickly, her cheeks heating. "But we don't need to find that out accidentally, either. We're returning to Earth, remember?"

His eyes went to TeShawna, and he bowed his head. "I cannot forget."

"And we don't want anything *unexpected* showing up once we get there," she said firmly. "A half-Cire child would not be treated well on our planet." She shuddered to even think what would happen if the government got involved.

"I understand. Most Cires are not forgiving of differences either." He finally dragged his eyes away from TeShawna. "You wish for something to prevent pregnancy?"

"I think it would be smart, yeah. Elaina and Jedan are sharing a cabin."

"So are you and Hrebec."

Her cheeks were definitely hot now. "Nothing has happened between us," she said quickly, then sighed. "But if there's one thing I preach to my girls, it's that it only takes one slip. It's better to be prepared."

"Are you at a fertile time?"

She did a quick calculation in her head and decided she must be about three weeks into her cycle. "I should be past it for this month. Why?"

"I would like to take a blood sample."

"Great." She made a face but held out her arm. "Go ahead."

"It won't hurt," he assured her.

Remembering how easily he had injected the translators, she tried to be optimistic about the procedure. He was true to his word; she only felt a brush of cool air and a slight pressure before he pulled back with a small vial of blood.

"I will see what I can determine," he said, but as he took the vial to a counter, Abby noticed that his gaze wandered back to TeShawna. He placed the vial in another device and entered some information into its control panel.

"I think sooner—rather than later—would be best," she said, and he shot her an amused look.

"I will make it a top priority," he promised. "The spectrometer will perform the analysis while we talk. Did you wish to share your knowledge of childbirth now?"

"Sure."

He led the way to the back room, and Abby gasped when she saw Kwaret's battered face.

"What happened to you?" She whirled to confront

Mekoi. "I thought the Cires were civilized."

"They did not do this," Kwaret said quickly. "Commander Khaen was... unhappy to learn that I provided assistance to the Cires. Captain Hrebec and Medic Mekoi have graciously allowed me to remain here rather than returning to the brig."

"I'm so sorry you were hurt because you tried to help us."

Kwaret looked uncomfortable. "I was originally trained as a medic. However, my family determined that it would be more profitable for me to join this... trading mission."

Mekoi made a derogatory noise and Kwaret's shoulders hunched. TeShawna and Abby both glared at the doctor and he looked a little ashamed.

"Well, I'm glad you were on this mission, no matter how ill-intentioned it might have been," Abby said. "If it weren't for you, Tiana would have died. You've also been a big help here on the ship."

"He has been of assistance," Mekoi admitted. "Now, shall we discuss how human females give birth?"

Mama and the Alien Warrior

Chapter Twenty-One

W hen Abby left the lab with TeShawna a few hours later, there was a small packet burning a hole in her pocket. Mekoi's machine had provided him with an analysis and he had slipped the resulting pills to her before they left. He had also provided two bottles with different variations on the nutritional supplement for Cassie to try with Angel.

"What did the doc give you?" TeShawna asked curiously.

Her attitude had softened considerably while they were in the lab, and Abby had noticed that she and Mekoi seemed to gravitate towards each other. By the time the women were ready to leave, his tail had been wrapped around TeShawna's wrist for quite a while. The girl had looked almost startled when she went to leave and seemed to notice it for the first time, but Abby saw her give it a quick stroke before she unwound it from around her wrist.

Now she tried to bluff. "What, the bottles? Those are for Cassie."

"Not those. What you put in your pocket."

Abby sighed. She had intended to discuss birth control with Hrebec first and then bring up the subject later with the girls, but TeShawna's sharp eyes put an end to that idea.

Resigned, she pulled out the packet and showed her the four small white pills. "Mekoi said they would act as birth control pills."

"Why, Miss Abby, you dog!" TeShawna gave her a look of mixed admiration and jealousy.

"I don't know that I'll need one, but you know what I

always say..."

"Better safe than sorry," TeShawna recited wryly. "But won't you need more than four?"

"He said each one would be good for at least six months, perhaps longer."

"Then why do you need four? Oh." TeShawna blushed, her cheeks darkening. "I don't need one of those things."

"Can you honestly tell me that you don't have any feelings for Dr. Mekoi?"

The blush intensified. "He's an alien. A bossy older alien."

"And?"

"I guess he's all right. That body sure don't look old."

Abby didn't say anything, waiting patiently.

"Oh, fine. I like him, okay? Even if he did get all jealous for no reason," the girl finally muttered.

"I don't think they have a lot of experience with women," Abby said thoughtfully. "He didn't understand that you were just being friendly."

TeShawna's eyes widened. "No experience? You mean he's a virgin?"

"I don't know, but remember that they don't have any women? He wouldn't have had many opportunities."

"A virgin? Who'd a thunk? But yeah, I can work with that. Train him up right." Her smile turned dreamy before she saw Abby looking at her. "Not that I'm planning on doing nothing... Fuck, give me one of them pills."

Abby handed it over, praying that Mekoi's machine was as accurate as he claimed. When she retrieved Lucie, she passed one along to Cassie as well.

Cassie frowned at the little pill. "These aliens are

nice enough, sure, but I'm not interested in them. Or any other man, for that matter," she said with a shudder. "I'd be just fine if no man ever laid a finger on me again."

Abby bit her lip. She knew that Cassie had been abused, but her contempt for the male gender troubled her. "I understand where you're coming from, but not all men are bad. You can't judge everyone based on your past experiences."

The words echoed in her own head. Didn't she have the tendency to do the same thing? But this wasn't about her and she gave Cassie a concerned look.

"No?" Cassie shook her head. "I'll admit that these guys seem all right, but I still don't know them." She grabbed a pill. "Better to be safe than sorry. Just in case."

Once Abby had Lucie and Tiana settled in the cabin, she knocked on the door next to hers.

Elaina opened the door, blushing when she saw Abby outside. "Oh, hi, Miss Abby. I was planning on coming to talk to you."

She stepped to one side and Abby could see that she'd followed Abby's lead. Both babies napped in bassinets made out of the large storage containers. The room was smaller than Hrebec's, with only a small seating area in front of the bed—the only bed.

Elaina's blush deepened when she saw where Abby's gaze settled. "It's not like you think. He's just helpin' me with the babies."

"But you want to be here, don't you?"

"Yeah." The girl turned away, fussing with a blanket. "I've never known anyone like him. Well, duh, I know he's an alien, but he's just so sweet. And big. Kinda makes me feel safe, you know?"

"I know." Abby knew only too well how good it felt to be tucked up against Hrebec's big body. She sighed and showed Elaina one of the pills. "This is a birth control pill. It should be good until we get back to Earth."

"Back to Earth? But we're not goin' there yet, right?"

"No. It could be another three or four weeks."

"Good." She blushed again. "I mean, it'll be nice to have the help." She looked at the pill but didn't take it. "But it's not like that between us. He hasn't even kissed me."

"I understand, and I'm certainly not encouraging you to do anything you don't want to do, but just in case?"

Elaina hesitated, then took the pill. "Is it a problem that I'm nursin'?"

"Dr. Mekoi said it wasn't."

"Are you taking one?"

It was a natural question, but Abby hesitated, surprisingly reluctant to discuss her feelings about Hrebec. Still, she'd never lied to the girls and she wasn't going to start now.

"Yes, I am. I don't know that I need it, but..."

"Better safe than sorry," Elaina finished.

"I guess I may have said that once or twice." Abby laughed. "I'll see you at dinner."

Unlike the previous night, when they gathered for the evening meal, she didn't try and segregate anyone. Ribel wasn't there, and after one hopeful glance around, Molly collapsed at one end of the table and didn't speak. Mekoi walked up to TeShawna and offered his hand to her with a bow. Her back straightened, and for a moment, Abby thought she would deny him, but then her face softened and she took his hand. Amber and Cassie were both surrounded by admiring young males, but Abby didn't see any signs of the previous night's rivalry. Many of the babies napped in makeshift bassinets, and the crew members were almost as fascinated by them as they were by the women.

Lucie introduced Abby to Inzen, the chief engineer who had provided her game. After a brief conversation, she saw his eyes move to Cassie. Despite the more relaxed atmosphere, Cassie appeared uncomfortable surrounded by the group of men.

Inzen scowled. "Young fools. Can't they tell the girl doesn't want 'em so close?"

"She's had a... difficult past," Abby explained.

"Puts on a brave face, though." Fleeting sorrow crossed his face. "Kind of reminds me of my daughter."

"Your daughter?" Shocked, Abby took a second look at Inzen. This time, she noticed the thickness of his ridges and the number of markings and realized that he must be considerably older than Hrebec.

"Red Death took her, too. She was one of the last. I hoped and prayed that she would be spared, but in the end..."

"I'm so sorry." Impulsively, she took his hand and squeezed it.

His tail patted her hand for the briefest instant before he cleared his throat. "I'll go keep an eye on the girl."

"Thank you."

She watched as he walked over to Cassie, dispersing the group surrounding her with a few well-chosen words. She couldn't hear what he said, but judging by the abashed expressions, he hadn't held back. Cassie gave him a grateful smile, and he started talking to her, careful to keep an easy distance between them.

"Why did you touch Inzen?" Hrebec growled next to her ear, and she jumped. She hadn't heard him approach. He loomed over her, cradling a sleeping Tiana in a one-handed football hold.

"Because I was sorry about his daughter." Her chin went up. "Why does it matter?"

"I don't like seeing another man's hands on you. Or his tail."

Abby repressed an eye roll as his own tail wrapped around her waist and tugged her to his side. The easy strength he used did nothing to alleviate the arousal that bubbled beneath her skin. His scent enveloped her, and she suddenly felt breathless.

He took a deep breath and his tail tightened possessively. "I can scent your arousal." His voice deepened. "I'm looking forward to our hankee pankee."

She was definitely blushing now, and her annoyance disappeared in a blaze of lust.

His eyes heated, and for a moment she thought he would kiss her right there in front of everyone. But then Lucie came running up and the moment was lost.

Despite her constant awareness of Hrebec seated next to her, dinner was very pleasant. Inzen watched over Cassie and Amber, while TeShawna and Mekoi focused on each other. Elaina and Jedan looked like a perfect family as they concentrated on the two babies, although Abby suspected that she and Hrebec and the girls presented the same image. The only unhappy person was Molly.

"I'm worried about her," she said to Hrebec while Lucie was distracted.

He followed her gaze and sighed. "I'm afraid Ribel is in the same state. The mating bond is difficult to overcome."

"What do you mean mating bond? There's no bond.

166

They haven't done anything yet." *She hoped.*

To the best of her knowledge, Molly had only ever been alone with him the one time, when he had told her that they couldn't have a relationship.

"A mating bond is much more than just a physical relationship." He looked at her. "You can feel the connection with the other person, even if the relationship is never consummated."

Well, shoot. Where exactly did that leave her and Hrebec? She thought back to her attraction to his scent and the faint hint of repulsion when confronted with another's, her desire to be with him, and just a general feeling of rightness when he was with her. Even as she had gone about her business this afternoon, part of her had been searching for his presence, and her only comfort was knowing that he was on the ship.

Would she continue to feel the same way when she was back on Earth? Would no man ever feel right? For now, her life revolved around Lucie and the girls, but some part of her had assumed that someday, in the future, she might meet someone. She had never thought it would be an alien captain.

"But it's not permanent, right?" She searched his expression for reassurance. "They'll both get over it once they're apart."

Hrebec hesitated. "I do not know how it will work for a human."

"How does it work for a Cire?"

"Mating bonds are permanent," he said, a touch of longing in his voice. "But I do not know at what point that occurs."

"But it's not through—" she lowered her voice even more. "Not through sex?"

"I have had sex before," he reminded her. "I felt no bond then."

He had told her that previously, so why did she feel there was something he wasn't telling her?

Tiana had been resting quietly against Hrebec's chest, big eyes taking in her surroundings, but now she started moving her head and rooting against his chest.

He stiffened as his eyes widened in alarm. "What's wrong with her?"

Abby couldn't help but smile. She loved Hrebec's determination to be a good father. "She's hungry. Do you want to feed her here or go back to the cabin?"

"Let us return to our cabin."

As he rose to his feet, Inzen appeared at his elbow. "Captain, may I speak to you?"

Hrebec gave the older man an irritated look as he began to move past him. "I was about to feed our—my daughter."

Inzen moved with him. "It will only take a moment."

Hrebec squared his massive shoulders and scowled at his chief engineer, but she stepped forward and reached for Tiana. "Hrebec, it's all right. I'll get her bottle ready."

Glancing down at Tiana, his expression softened. His hold on the baby tightened—a quick hug—before he passed Tiana to her. His tail swept over the baby's head, caressing Abby's hand as well.

"Thank you, Abigail," he said, his dark eyes holding her in a steady gaze.

"Go ahead," she said reassuringly. "We'll see you soon."

Chapter Twenty-Two

I nzen was as good as his word. When Hrebec returned, Abby had just finished preparing Tiana's bottle and was trying to supervise Lucie's bedtime preparations. Unfortunately, Lucie was objecting to everything. She didn't want to take a shower; she wanted a bath. She didn't want her pink jammies; she wanted her new white ones. She didn't want Abby; she wanted Hrebec.

As soon as he walked in, Lucie threw herself at him. He had entered the room looking more solemn than she'd seen him since their very first encounter, but when Lucie rushed over and hugged his legs, his face softened.

His tail curled about Lucie, hugging her back. "What's the matter, little one?"

Lucie mumbled into his legs. "Mama's being mean."

"I don't believe that for a minute," he said firmly.

Abby sighed. "She doesn't want to get ready for bed."

He lowered himself onto one knee before Lucie. "But if you don't get ready for bed, I can't tell you a story."

"A story?" Her eyes went big.

"Yes, but only once you're all clean and tucked into bed."

"I's can do that!"

"That's a good girl." He kissed her head before she danced off towards the bedroom.

"You do have a knack with her." Abby shook her head while she handed him Tiana and the bottle. "Will you feed her while I go supervise Lucie before she sets the ship afloat?"

"What if she won't take it from me?"

"Here, try this." She handed him her cardigan. "Wrap it around her first."

"You think it's scent?"

"I think that's part of it." The sound of running water came from the other room. "I have to check on Lucie. If it doesn't work, I won't be long."

Feeling slightly guilty, she abandoned him to his fate. However, by the time she had Lucie in her pajamas and into bed, he joined them with a triumphant smile.

"She took the bottle."

"I'm so glad." And she was, but a part of her was also a little sad that Tiana was already learning to live without her. She had to, she reminded herself, but it warmed her heart when she took the baby from him and Tiana gave her a wide, toothless grin.

While she rocked the baby to sleep, Hrebec told Lucie about another princess, a brave one who had to travel to a new land and leave her friends behind to save her people. She wondered if he was trying to prepare Lucie for the inevitable. Her own throat grew tight at the thought.

She pulled Tiana closer and couldn't help but give a longing look at Hrebec, his big body so strong yet so gentle as he settled Lucie under the covers. He looked up and their eyes met, his own yearning crystal clear in those strange dark eyes. The lump in her throat expanded, but she dragged her gaze away and went to put the now sleeping Tiana in her bassinet. Hrebec followed her silently into the next room as she closed the door behind them.

"I think I would like a drink tonight," Abby blurted out as soon as they were alone.

"Of course, my flower." He went to the small bar

and poured her a drink. "Are you worried? I hope you know I would never force myself on you."

"Of course I know that." She took the liquor and sat down on the couch. "I guess I'm just nervous."

He frowned and poured himself a small glass. "I thought you were anticipating our time together."

"I was. I mean, I am. It's just…". She twisted her fingers together nervously. He sat down next to her, covering her restless movements with one big, warm hand. His touch—and his scent—soothed her and she took a deep breath. "I don't know *why* I'm so nervous."

"Would you prefer to do something else? Do your people play card games?"

His question startled her out of her panic. "You want to play cards? Now?"

"Oh no, my flower. I want to remove this very tempting outfit and worship your body. To caress your delightful breasts and to sate my thirst with your delicious cunt." He leaned closer, his tail snaking around to hold her. "I have thought of nothing else since we parted. My shaft has wept for you."

He drew her hand to his lap, holding it to the massive erection straining against the tight uniform, and she could feel the dampness. Her own desire came flooding back, washing away her doubts. Her hand tightened around him. He moaned, and she realized that his tail had wound itself between her legs, pressing against her rapidly hardening clit.

"Oh my." She stroked him through his pants, shivering with anticipation as she felt the wide, pebbled shaft.

He cleared his throat. "So, no cards?"

When she looked up at him in shock, he covered her

mouth with his, his tongue probing urgently. She opened to him, delighting in his delicious lemony taste, her body melting into his. One big hand held her head in place for his kiss as he delved deeper, his other working feverishly at her breasts while his tail massaged her swollen clit.

He made an impatient noise and pulled her onto his lap, surrounding her with his body, his scent. She clasped his neck, trying to pull him even closer as she writhed against him. There was a ripping noise and then her pants were gone, nothing separating her from the pebbled surface of his tail as it rubbed and kneaded, sliding through her slickness and pressing up into her needy channel. She convulsed, and he swallowed her cries of pleasure as she came in a long shuddering wave.

When she finally stopped shaking, he lifted his head and smiled. "Most certainly that is better than cards."

"Mm. You're right." She stretched in satisfaction, and the movement reminded her of the massive erection throbbing beneath her butt.

Time to decide. Although she knew he would never pressure her, she wasn't cruel enough to stop after coming so far. There was always the possibility of another blowjob, but gazing up into that strange, handsome alien face, she knew what she wanted.

She took a deep breath. "I asked Dr. Mekoi for a birth control pill today."

"I know you did," he said solemnly. "He didn't tell me, but Cassie told Inzen about the pills and he told me."

"Is that why he wanted to talk to you?"

He hesitated. "Yes."

She narrowed her eyes at his hesitation. "Is that all?"

"No, my flower. The rest was… personal."

An unexpected feeling of hurt flashed through her.

She was half-naked in his arms. Was that somehow *not* personal?

He must have seen her withdrawal because before she could stiffen, he pulled her closer and kissed her gently. "I didn't intend to distress you. In fact, it is the opposite. Can you believe that my only intention is to prevent you from feeling distress?"

Could she?

Looking up at his worried face again, she nodded slowly. "Yes, I trust you."

And she did. The one man she found to believe in, and he was an alien who she'd encountered millions of miles from home.

"Thank you, my flower."

He bent his head and kissed her again—a kiss that started off as a sweet acknowledgment and rapidly became deeply carnal.

"I want you inside me, Hrebec," she gasped, her hand already reaching for him.

"I have not yet tasted your sweet cunt."

"Later." She fumbled with his pants. "Dammit, how do you get these things open?"

With one lightning fast move, he removed her top and laid her back on the couch before stripping away his own clothes. Her breath caught in nervous excitement—there was just so much of him, all of it big and green and hard, with those tantalizing nubs that had her pussy aching in anticipation. His cock was wide and thick, narrowing slightly between the heavy base and wide tip. She licked her lips and saw a pearl of precum appear on the broad head.

"Come to me, Hrebec." She opened her arms and he lowered himself over her.

They both groaned as his head sought her entrance

and he pushed gently. Despite the slickness coating her lips, her body resisted.

"Open for me, my flower," he urged, maintaining a slow, insistent pressure until her body opened and he slid partially inside. The immediate stretch had her pussy fluttering wildly as it tried to cope with his invasion. The feeling skirted the edge of pain, but then his tail stroked across her clit and the pressure became pleasure.

He paused, and she thought he was waiting for her to adjust, but when she tried to raise her hips and encourage him, he shuddered then stiffened. She looked up to find his face taut and his attention locked on the place where they were joined.

"Hrebec, is something wrong?"

"No." Even his voice sounded strained. "I want to be inside you more than anything I've ever wanted."

"I want that too." She tried to wiggle her hips again.

He groaned and his eyes closed. "Once I'm inside you, I will knot."

"Is that a bad thing? You said you would find fulfillment that way." She bit her lip. "Is it… dangerous?"

"For you? No." He flexed his hips and pushed inside another inch. "Your cunt is like a silken fist, impossibly tight, but you will stretch to take me."

Desperate for more of that overwhelming stretch, she lifted her hips again and gained another inch. "Hrebec."

He opened his eyes and gazed at her. "I choose you, Abigail. I choose this. Remember that."

"Yes, I choose you too. Now move, please."

He did, burying himself deep inside in one hard plunge that set every one of her senses on fire. Her breath came in rapid pants as she tried to adjust to the incredible fullness. He started to pull back and she felt the ribbed surface of his cock rubbing against the sensitive tissues, creating sparks of pleasure just as his tail vibrated against her clit.

With a wailing cry that he once again covered with his mouth, she came, her body spasming in almost painful waves around the massive intrusion. Her body arched and shook as he kissed her frantically, barely waiting for her tremors to subside before he was plunging into her in urgent haste, stretching her wider still, forcing her to take more until he buried his own cries in her mouth. She felt him swell inside of her, the base of his cock expanding inside the depths of her channel and sending her into another quaking orgasm as she felt his hot seed flowing into her.

His mouth finally left hers as he buried his head in the crook of her neck and she tightened her arms around him. They held each other until her pulse slowed and she could catch her breath.

When Hrebec raised his head, his face was serene, the strain completely gone. "You are everything I hoped for, Abigail. I—"

Her breath caught. "You?"

He closed his eyes briefly, then shook his head. "I do not know how long I will remain like this."

"Mm." She wiggled experimentally and gasped as the movement reawakened the sensitive tissues. The stretching fullness had not diminished, which sent a shiver jolting down her spine. He reached down between their bodies and ran his thumb across her clit. Her body instinctively tried to tighten, only to meet the barrier of his cock.

He groaned appreciatively. "This is a most exquisite agony."

He repeated the stroke and she could already feel her

climax building again.

"Can you come again?" she asked breathlessly, her hands tightening on his shoulders as his tail came up and began to tease her nipples.

"No. But you will." His eyes glowed with heat. "Many times."

Chapter Twenty-Three

By the time his shaft finally softened, Abigail was limp and helpless in Hrebec's arms. He carefully pulled free and gathered her close to him. The couch was too small to be comfortable, but he didn't care; he was too overcome with emotion to want to move.

He had found his mate, his woman.

Inzen had warned him that if he knotted inside her, he would be bound to her. There would be no other female for him. Even though he knew he wouldn't be able to keep Abigail, in the end, it had been an easy decision. He would rather have her for this brief time, to know the bliss of having found his mate, than spend his life alone without ever knowing this sense of completion. Basking in the happiness of being with his mate, he buried his nose in her hair and let their combined scents fill him.

Abigail finally stirred. "We should go to bed."

"Wait here. I will tend to you."

He pulled on his pants, then walked quietly through the bedroom to fetch a shirt for her to sleep in and a cleansing cloth. There was something deeply satisfying in seeing their combined fluids as he gently cleansed her reddened folds. She blushed as he wiped her clean, wincing a little despite his gentleness.

"Was the knotting too much for you, my mate?" he asked.

Abigail's eyes flew open. "What did you say?"

"I'm sorry. I didn't think before I spoke."

"Hrebec, you know I have to return to Earth."

"Yes, of course." He did understand, even though the reminder filled him with sorrow. "You have your responsibilities, and I have mine."

"I wish... In many ways, I wish I could stay with you."

He smoothed the worried line between her brows with the touch of his finger. "I told you that I understood."

Without waiting for a response, he lifted her into his arms and took her to bed. As usual, Lucie was sprawled sideways across the bed. After gently depositing Abigail, he straightened Lucie out.

With his heart full, he slipped into bed beside his mate. Tiana was close at hand, sleeping in her bassinet, but he didn't reach for her. Tonight, he wanted his mate in his arms that he might savor every moment they had together. He wrapped his arms and tail around her and she gave a sleepy sigh and nestled back against him. Instead of thinking about the future, he let himself drift off to sleep, content with the present.

For once, Lucie was not the first to awaken. Instead, Hrebec opened his eyes to find the room in stillness. Abigail was still in his arms, her soft weight and sweet scent causing his cock to thicken. If they had been alone, he would not hesitate to part her legs and feast on her delicious cunt.

However, they weren't alone. Lucie's tiny feet dug into his ribs, and he silently praised Granthar that humans didn't possess talons. Despite his aching cock, waking up this way pleased him immensely. He had his family around him. Even as he smiled at the thought, he heard Tiana stir. Little snuffling noises came from the bassinet, and he realized with delight that he knew her well enough now to recognize that she was hungry.

Reluctantly disentangling himself from Abigail, he

slipped out of bed and picked up the infant. Her eyes were open and she cooed at him as he picked her up, her head nuzzling into his arm in a contented gesture. As quietly as possible, he prepared her bottle and took her into the front room to change and feed her. He had forgotten to pick up the cardigan, but it didn't seem to matter. She latched on to the bottle eagerly and began feeding, her tail curled around his wrist.

As his tail stroked her smooth little head, his arms ached despite her slight weight. All those years ago, if he had only known that this was all it took: holding them. The Cires had been so desperate to save themselves that they set their children apart, confining them to sterile incubators rather than embracing each precious little life. And it shocked him to his core that having Tiana in his arms now kept him from sinking into guilt and sorrow over all those lost lives. Because with Tiana, he had been able to save someone.

A soft noise drew his attention to the doorway. Abigail stood there, looking sleepy and adorable.

"You didn't need the cardigan," she said a little sadly.

"No, my flower." He held out his free hand, and she came and joined him on the couch, curling against his side as they both watched Tiana. "I suspect it is no longer necessary."

Her lips trembled as she tried to smile. "Good. That's good. She doesn't need me anymore."

"I don't think that's it." He looked down at the infant to see that her eyes were focused on Abigail. "After last night, our scents are mingled. I believe that she has accepted me because of that."

"But that's temporary, right? What happens when it wears off?"

He suspected that would never happen—that Abigail was a part of him now—but he didn't mention it.

Instead, he shrugged lightly. "Hopefully, by then she will have grown accustomed to my scent as well."

"I was thinking about that yesterday," she said slowly. "What if that's something else your babies need to thrive? They bond—imprint—on their first caregiver. Perhaps your labs should add that to the other things they are trying."

He stroked Tiana's tiny tail where it wrapped around his wrist as he considered what Abigail had said. The infants needed more than just physical contact; they needed a bond with their caregivers.

"It had not occurred to me," he admitted, "but given the way Tiana has reacted, that is an excellent suggestion. I will send a message to see if it would be possible to assign a specific person to each group of infants."

Pleased as he was with his mate's suggestion, he found he was not as excited as he should have been. Of course, he wanted his people to continue, but his thoughts were no longer concerned with their fate, but with his new family.

"You's left me." Now Lucie stood in the doorway, an accusatory look on her face.

"Just letting you sleep, baby," Abigail said, holding out her arms.

Lucie pouted but came over and curled up in Abigail's lap. His tail wrapped around them both, pulling them into his side while he fed Tiana. Immense contentment filled him as they sat together in the quiet room.

"What do you plan to do today?" he asked at last.

Abigail sighed. "I'm not sure. I still have a little more sewing to do, but I'm almost done. At home, I work with the girls on various things—learning household skills, financial planning, educational programs, whatever they need to prepare them to take care of themselves and their children."

"That is most admirable." Abigail's role in the lives of her girls was similar to his duty to his young crew members.

"It's why I started the home to begin with. To give girls with few alternatives a safe place to give birth and get a head start on a better life."

"Chores and school first, then naps, then play time," Lucie piped up, and Abigail laughed.

"That's right, baby." She smiled at the little girl, then looked at him. "I've found that a routine helps the girls. We also make dinner together."

"Would you like to do that tonight?" He only hoped that Pravit's tolerance towards Lucie would extend to the rest of the females.

"Maybe. Everyone has their hands full with the extra babies, but it might be nice to help Pravit. If he doesn't mind, of course."

"I likes Pravit," Lucie said. "I wants to help him!"

"Just because you help him doesn't mean you get any pastries," Abigail warned.

Lucie's face fell. "None at all?"

"You can have one, and that's only if you're good."

"Okay," she sighed, then smiled. "I likes his stories, too."

Tiana had finished her bottle and dozed in his arms. He burped her as Abigail had shown him before he asked, "Do you have the cloth for the sling?"

"Are you going to take her again?"

"Yes. As you suggested, I want her to get

accustomed to me."

"You're right. But maybe I can have a turn with her after lunch." She bit her lip. "I won't have much time left with her."

"Yes, my flower. I think she needs us both." He only prayed that Tiana would continue to thrive once Abigail left them.

Abigail arranged the cloth again, wrapping Tiana snugly against his chest. As he prepared to leave, he hesitated, then gathered Abigail close and kissed her as thoroughly as possible, given Lucie's watchful eyes. He ran his eyes over her, pleased with the results. Abigail's cheeks were pink and he could see the hard points of her nipples.

Lucie giggled and danced around them. "You's kissed Mama again!"

"Yes, I did," he agreed. "I will probably do it again as well."

"Kiss me, too, Papa," she demanded, holding up her little arms.

He froze in place, joy and sorrow warring in his heart. Abigail bit her lip again, the beautiful pink color completely draining from her face.

Hrebec knelt down so that he was at Lucie's level and wrapped his tail around her. "Little one, why did you call me that?"

"You's Tiana's papa. I heard you say." Her eyes were wide and anxious. "And me and Tiana is sisters so you's my papa too."

"But Leonardo is your special name for me. I would miss it if you didn't call me that." His statement was true, but he hadn't realized until he'd heard Lucie say it, how much it would mean to him to have her think of him as her father.

Her bottom lip trembled, and he gave Abigail a helpless look.

She had recovered her composure enough to kneel beside them and put an arm around Lucie. "Why don't we talk about this later? Hrebec has to go to work, baby."

"I wants to go with him," Lucie pouted.

"Why don't you come with me after the mid-shift meal?" he suggested. "Just like yesterday."

"Can we see the pink show again?"

"Yes, little one."

"I 'spose." She gave a big sigh before her cheery little smile finally peeked out.

He hugged her, relieved when her small arms went around his neck and she gave him a sloppy kiss on his cheek.

Mama and the Alien Warrior

Chapter Twenty-Four

This time, there were no surprised looks when Hrebec carried Tiana onto the bridge, but throughout the morning, his thoughts kept drifting back to Lucie calling him her papa. He'd spent all those years fighting to preserve his species, but it had never been personal. This—this desire for a family of his own—tore at his heart in a completely new way, although it seemed just as hopeless. At least he would have Tiana. Still, it wasn't until he joined Abigail and Lucie for the mid-shift that he truly felt complete.

After the meal, he took Lucie to the bridge again. She insisted on sitting on his shoulder to watch the "pink show" as she peppered him with questions. He did his best to explain interstellar travel at a level that a four-year-old could understand. He failed miserably, and once again, Inzen came to the rescue. The man had a natural gift with children, and Hrebec remembered that he'd had a daughter of his own.

After he'd returned Lucie to their cabin for her nap—and spent a few delightful minutes kissing Abigail—he returned to the bridge and drew Inzen aside.

"I was wondering..." he said slowly.

"Yes, Captain?"

"If you had known how it would end, would you still have wished for a child?"

"Yes," he said without hesitation. "Even if I'd had only a single day with Zentia, it would still be worth it. She and my mate were everything to me."

"And you lost them both."

"Yes. It is a pain that never goes away, Hrebec, but I would never give up my time with them."

"You never considered using the memory eraser?"

"No." He gave Hrebec a shrewd look. "Everyone copes with grief in different ways, but I suspect you will never make that decision either."

Hrebec nodded and turned the subject to their remaining flight. Deep down, he already knew that Inzen was right. When he had considered using the memory eraser before, he had been overwhelmed by his sense of failure and despair. Abigail and Lucie did not cause him despair, only a happiness that he would never choose to forget, no matter how much pain his memories would cause.

He found that he did not want to be away from his family in the short time that he had left, and he made an excuse to join them as they prepared the evening meal. Pravit grumped and scowled, but he obviously enjoyed having the females in his kitchen. Lucie bounced around excitedly while sneaking more than one pastry, but he didn't have the heart to scold her. Even if Abigail had not been his mate, he would have been impressed by the way she worked with her females, directing their tasks with firm patience and easy laughter.

The resulting meal was delicious, and once again, dinner proved to be a relaxed occasion. He and Jedan had set up a schedule so that each of the younger crew members had a chance to encounter the human females, and he was pleased to see that they had taken his words to heart. His warriors remained polite and respectful despite their obvious awe.

As he fed Tiana, he noticed that two of the females also used bottles to feed their infants.

"You have switched to the nutritional formulas?" he asked Abigail.

"Yes. Cassie wanted to be able to feed her baby

herself, and Amber volunteered to feed Lily so that TeShawna could concentrate on her own daughter." She looked at Jedan, who was intently focused on Ginger, and laughed. "I think Jedan may encourage Elaina to let him try bottle-feeding soon as well."

"It is a... special feeling to provide for one's child," he agreed.

He thought of mentioning to Jedan that continuing to bond with Elaina's children might add to his sorrow when he was separated from them, but he decided that the man must make his own decisions.

The only dark spot was the youngest pregnant female. Her pale face and despondent posture worried him. She had taken only a minimal role in the meal preparation, apathetically feeding chunks of vegetables into a slicer. Abigail, too, gave the girl concerned glances and left him for a while to cajole the girl into eating a few bites.

"I'm so worried about her," she said when she returned. "I'm almost ready to throw one of Ribel's shirts over her and see if that will make her eat."

His young ensign had chosen to stay away from the females entirely, deliberately taking other assignments during meal times, but Hrebec had noticed that he also looked pale and unhappy.

"Perhaps we should consider letting them spend some time together," he said hesitantly.

"What if it makes it worse?"

"Could it be much worse?"

She followed his gaze and shook her head. "I don't know. You might be right. I thought she would have moved on to someone else by now. Honestly, I'm surprised she wasn't attracted to Inzen." His chief engineer stood next to Cassie, holding Angel carefully and beaming with delight.

"He has that older, protective air she's always responded to in the past."

"If it is a true bond, there is no substitution."

She looked up at him, her eyes glistening with unspoken emotion. "I know, Hrebec. I know."

The evening passed in a blur of bottles and bedtimes stories, in what he recognized had already become a familiar routine. His chest ached as he finally joined Abigail in the front room after they took turns preparing for bed. Despite that, his body responded immediately to the sight of her waiting for him, dressed once again in the alluring white nightgown.

"You are a vision of loveliness, my ma... my flower."

He knew she caught his slip, but she let it go, surveying him appreciatively as she scanned his bare chest and the loose sleep pants that did nothing to disguise his erection.

"You look pretty good yourself."

Joining her on the couch, he pulled her onto his lap and kissed her until all he could taste was her, until he felt her essence surrounding him. She squirmed against him, rubbing the hard points of her nipples against his chest. He lowered her back so he could take a turn teasing the tempting peaks, while his tail slipped under her gown. The narrow dimensions of the furniture didn't allow him to spread her out as fully as he wished.

"I need a larger couch," he said, thinking somewhat wistfully of the big bed in the next room.

"Or a bed we don't share," she agreed, arching her back as his tail teased her swollen clit.

"Yes. As much as I love having my fam... having all

of you with me, it would be nice to sleep with you alone in my arms, so that I could turn to you in the night and wake you with pleasure."

Damn, his feelings kept trying to slip out and once again, he knew that she had noticed. She didn't say anything, simply raising her hand to caress the lamella curving back across his skull.

Determined to ignore the ache in his throat, he moved off the couch, kneeling in front of her and using his shoulders to part her legs. Her delicate folds glistened, flushed with arousal, but he could see that the sensitive flesh was reddened. He probed gently at her tiny entrance and she quivered.

"Are you sore, Abigail?"

"Maybe a little," she admitted. He pushed his finger deeper inside the snug sheath of her body. As tightly as she gripped the single digit, it seemed impossible that his cock had ever managed to penetrate the narrow passage. "But that feels amazing. Please don't stop."

"Never."

He licked the length of her tempting slit, her taste flooding his senses. His cock ached, longing to be buried inside all of that delicious sweetness, but he ignored it. Even though their time together was short, he would not take the chance of harming her delicate body. She needed time to recover. Tonight, he would be satisfied with bringing her pleasure.

His mouth fastened over her clit, circling and tugging, as his finger stroked gently in and out and his tail echoed his actions, teasing and plucking her taut nipples until she trembled beneath him, her hands clutching his skull in mindless pleasure. As her tremors subsided, he kissed his way up her body, pausing to feast on her nipples, until they too were pink and swollen, before finally reaching the delectable haven of her mouth.

Her tongue dueled with his as he devoured her, desperate for every morsel of her sweetness. His cock came to rest between her legs, and he gave into temptation, sliding it back and forth between the slickened folds. She curled her legs around his hips, lifting against him to increase the pressure. His tail followed, dipping briefly into the tiny, tempting entrance that he could not—would not—enter, before the lubricated tip probed at her second small hole. She gasped into his mouth but didn't protest. As he breached the tight ring of muscle, the pressure against his tail's sensitive tip had him ejaculating in one long heated wave, while she cried out a second time into his mouth and he felt her climax beneath him.

While it couldn't compare to the ecstasy of being actually buried inside her luscious body, it was deeply satisfying to climax in her arms. He raised his head and smiled at the sight of her heavy lids and flushed cheeks. By Granthar, he adored seeing her pink with pleasure.

Dropping another quick kiss to her lips, he stood up and removed his now dampened sleep pants. With some reluctance, he cleaned his fluids from her body. Returning to his original seat, he lifted her back on to his lap. She snuggled closer, but instead of drifting off to sleep as he expected, she started playing with his fingers thoughtfully.

"Is something troubling you, my flower?"

She took a deep breath before she looked up at him, her pale eyes dark with concern. "I'm worried that Lucie is growing too attached to you."

"Attached? I do not understand. She is not fastened to me."

"It means she's very fond of you."

"I see. I have grown very attached to her as well." He cupped her face. "To all of you."

"I feel the same way. You know I do."

His chest ached. "Do you really, Abigail?"

"Of course, I do. You're the finest man I've ever known. I—" She bit back her words and looked away, forcing a smile as she ran a hand down his chest. "And you definitely have the finest body."

"Thank you. I find yours most delightful as well." Despite his immediate response to her touch, he refused to accept her change of subject. "Are you scared of how you feel? Of how Lucie feels?"

"Yes, I'm scared. I'm going to go home and never see you again, and I don't think any man will ever match up to my memory of you."

"There is a machine," he said reluctantly. "It will erase this portion of time from your memory. It has been strongly suggested by the High Council that it be used on all of you when you are returned to Earth. They feel that your planet is not ready for the knowledge of our existence."

"None of us would ever say a word about this," she said indignantly, pulling away from him with a shake of her head. "Even if we did, they'd lock us up for being crazy."

"I know you wouldn't reveal anything. I would never force that upon you. I'm simply telling you that you could choose to forget."

"Forget this? Forget Tiana? Forget everything that has happened between us? No, Hrebec, I couldn't do that. No matter how much it hurts, I want to remember."

As she echoed his earlier thoughts, he could contain himself no longer. "I love you, Abigail."

Her eyes filled with tears. "Oh, Hrebec. I think I love you too. It's just that it's all been so fast... and so confusing."

"Shh, I know."

Using his tail, he pulled her back against his chest, his heart full. She had not denied her feelings for him. For now, it was enough.

Chapter Twenty-Five

Abby lay awake long after Hrebec carried her to bed. His arms were wrapped around her and his tail was a comforting weight across her stomach. He loved her. The knowledge filled her with a mixture of joy and sorrow. While she had told him that she wasn't sure, she had no real doubts that she felt the same way. If she had been the only one involved, she didn't think she would have hesitated to join her life with his and explore this strange new world at his side. But she wasn't the only one. She had a responsibility to the girls, of course, but even more, she had a responsibility to Lucie. What would become of her daughter in this alien environment? Lucie might want—possibly even need—a father, but she also needed a home, an education, and the promise of a future.

After a restless night, she awoke to find Lucie already dressed in her new pink dress and watching her anxiously.

The words rushed out of Lucie as soon as Abby's eyes opened. "We's coming to the planet and Leonardo says we can watch, but not 'til you wakes up and I can't wakes you."

"Guess I'm awake now," she said, smiling at her daughter.

"Yay!" she shrieked. "She's awake, Leonardo!"

"Softly, Lucie," Hrebec said, appearing in the doorway. Tiana was in his arms, feeding contentedly. "I can see that. Did you sleep well, my flower?"

"Well enough." She shrugged, pretending she didn't see the concern in his eyes. "We're arriving at Trevelor?"

"Yes. We'll be landing in about an hour. I thought

perhaps your females would enjoy seeing the approach. I have had a message sent to them."

"I'm sure they'll be thrilled. It will just take me a minute to get dressed."

She climbed out of bed as she spoke, and his eyes surveyed her appreciatively. "You are dressed most delightfully."

"Silly," Lucie giggled. "That's Mama's nightgown. She can't wear that outside!"

"No? I suppose you're right. I would not want anyone else to see how beautiful she looks."

"She'll feel a lot more beautiful after she's had a chance to wash her face and brush her teeth," Abby said firmly. "Lucie, did you brush your teeth?"

"Yes, Mama. See?" She opened her mouth wide. "Leonardo helped me, just like a papa would do."

Her words fell into a stricken silence, but Abby managed to clear her throat and respond. "I'm sure you did a good job, baby. Now scoot on out of here while I get ready."

A short time later, the four of them walked onto the bridge, and Abby couldn't help but gasp at the sight. It looked exactly like something out of a science fiction movie, from the consoles sparkling with colored lights to the wide screens that dominated the front of the room. On the center screen, she could see a planet approaching. Even though the continents weren't remotely similar to any pictures she had seen of Earth from space, the mixture of blues and greens was familiar enough to bring a lump to her throat.

"It's beautiful," she murmured.

"I believe it to be a very pleasant place," Hrebec

agreed. "Their population has always been low, but they didn't lose many to the Red Death, so their civilization remains intact."

"Isn't this cool, Miss Abby?" TeShawna asked.

She was standing to one side with Vanessa in her arms. Mekoi stood behind her, and Abby noticed that his tail was wrapped around TeShawna and the baby. She couldn't help wondering why they were together so early in the morning. Had they spent the night with him? Maybe it had been as inevitable as her ending up with Hrebec.

As she continued to look around, she saw that Jedan, Elaina, and their two babies were also present.

"Where's Cassie? Is she coming? Or Molly and Amber?"

"Cassie went to get Molly," TeShawna said frowning. "She didn't want to come and Amber didn't want to leave her, even though she wanted to see all this too. Cassie isn't going to put up with that sh—nonsense."

"I hope she can convince her. I'd hate for them to miss this."

The planet grew closer, filling the large screen, and she could begin to distinguish the many shades of green covering the land masses. The blues of the water were equally varied. In both the oceans and the many lakes that speckled the land, they ranged from a dark, almost purple color to a light and delicate turquoise.

"Here we are!" Cassie said from behind her. Despite her attempt to sound cheerful, Abby could hear the twinge of frustration in her voice.

"That's good," she said, turning to face them. All three girls stood in the entrance, Cassie and Amber with babies in their arms, while Molly drooped listlessly on one side. "Isn't this a magnificent sight?"

Cassie and Amber nodded, stepping forward in awestruck silence. At first, Abby thought Molly wasn't even going to look, but then her head came up. However, instead of looking at the screen, she searched the bridge, her eyes feverish. There was a crash at the far end of the bridge, but Abby didn't even need to look to know who was there. Molly took one step forward before her face turned white and she started to crumple.

Ribel lunged for her, pulling her into his arms with desperate urgency. "Molly, Molly! Speak to me, my mate."

Mekoi joined them, running a scanner over the unconscious girl. "I don't like this. She appears to be dehydrated and malnourished."

"This is your fault," Ribel snarled at Abby. "You separated us."

Hrebec stepped in front of Abby, every inch an intimidating warrior. "You will *never* speak to my mate that way."

Ribel dropped his head in shame. "I'm sorry. I just... Please help her, Mekoi."

"I will," the medic promised. "Bring her down to the lab."

No one stepped forward to take Molly away from Ribel, and Abbie didn't have the heart to suggest it.

"I think I'd better come, too," Amber said quietly as she sucked in a deep breath. "My water just broke."

The approaching planet was forgotten as the bridge erupted into confusion. Someone took Lily, and Inzen stepped forward, lifting Amber into his arms despite her weak protests that she could walk. Mekoi led the way out of the room on the run, Ribel and Inzen close behind.

"I have to go with them," Abby said.

"Go," Hrebec responded immediately. "I will take

care of our girls and the landing and join you as soon as possible."

"Thank you." She gave his hand a grateful squeeze and dashed off after her girls.

By the time the ship landed and Hrebec arrived at the lab, Amber's contractions were still mild and she was more excited than nervous. Abby left TeShawna with her in the newly created birthing room and went to speak to Hrebec.

"Where are the girls?" she asked.

"They are with Pravit." A grin fought its way through his concerned expression. "He is wearing Tiana in the sling and Lucie is trying to tell him how to make something called 'cookies.'"

"That's my girl." Abby managed a smile in return.

"How are the females?"

"Amber is a little anxious, but she's doing well." She looked into the other room, where Molly lay silently on Kwaret's bed. "Molly hasn't regained consciousness, although Dr. Mekoi is giving her internal fluids. He asked me if he should let Ribel stay, but I don't know what's best. She fainted at the sight of him."

"Let him stay. It was shock, not repulsion, that made her faint. She will take comfort in his presence, even if she is not consciously aware that he is there."

Abby nodded, relieved that she wouldn't have to make the poor man leave. He was crouched at Molly's side, whispering to her, his tail circling her wrist.

Hrebec frowned. "Where is the Vedeckian?"

"He's monitoring Amber while Mekoi is with Molly. Remember, he does have some experience with childbirth."

He opened his mouth, but Mekoi emerged from Molly's room and interrupted him.

"Have we landed?" Mekoi asked.

"Yes."

"We should contact their medical facility."

Abby's heart did a somersault in her chest. "What's wrong?"

"The female is still unconscious, but her pulse rate keeps spiking. I suspect that she is about to go into labor as well." His tail lashed anxiously. "I'm afraid that she will need more help than I can give her."

Hrebec nodded gravely as he focused on his communicator. "I will make arrangements immediately. Abigail, I assume you will wish to go with her?"

"Yes, of course." She looked into the other room where TeShawna was holding Amber's hand. "Should we take Amber, too?"

"I think it would be wise." Mekoi shrugged helplessly. "I believe I could handle the birth, but it would be better to have trained professionals involved."

"You will accompany them as well, Mekoi," Hrebec ordered.

"Of course. They are my patients."

"I will escort you," Hrebec said.

"But the girls..." Abby protested.

"They are fine with Pravit. I will escort you and make sure that conditions are satisfactory. Then I will return to the ship."

"Thank you." She couldn't help but be glad that she wouldn't be alone on a strange planet.

Hrebec's communicator beeped, and he checked the message.

"They are sending transport for the females. I will

meet them at the landing ramp." He stepped closer and lifted her chin. "Do not worry, Abigail. They will have the best of care."

He pressed his lips to hers, just a brief touch, and then he strode away.

Mama and the Alien Warrior

Chapter Twenty-Six

W hen Hrebec returned, a small group of Trevelorians accompanied him. Abby did her best not to stare, but she hadn't expected such obviously birdlike aliens. A crest of brightly colored feathers covered their heads and ran down across their shoulders. Their arms also were covered with feathers, much like wings, although they wouldn't have supported the plump bodies that hopped along on twiggy little legs.

The lead Trevelorian stopped and bowed to Abby. "I am L'chong Sardma, Chief Medic of the Wiang Birthing Center. Thank you for allowing us to render assistance."

"Thank you," she managed, but looking at his alien features, she wondered how much he could know about human births.

Something in her expression must have given away her concern, because he bowed a second time, his beaked nose quivering. "Do not worry. We have assisted with many births from many species."

"Oh, yes, of course. I'm sure you're... qualified," she said quickly.

The thin lips twisted and small black eyes twinkled at her. "You do not believe so presently, but you will see."

With swift efficiency, he reviewed their cases with Mekoi and arranged for Amber and Molly to be placed on the floating stretchers that he had brought with him.

Ribel stood next to Molly's stretcher, his jaw clenched. "I'm not leaving her."

"You may come," L'chong said.

Amber begged TeShawna to come as well, and after making sure that Cassie and Inzen could take care of

Vanessa as well as Angel and Lily, she agreed.

As they followed the stretchers, TeShawna edged closer to Abby. "Never thought I'd end up on an alien planet. What you think it'll be like?"

"It didn't seem that different from space," Abby said.

Although she was a little nervous herself, Hrebec was on her other side, and she knew he'd never let anything happen to her.

But when they stepped outside the ship, she realized that the view from space had been deceiving. This place was nothing like Earth.

The sky overhead was blue, but not the familiar Earth blue; instead, it was a brilliant turquoise. The trees were more like incredibly tall grasses, multi-trunked and swaying gently in the soft breeze, and in an array of colors that, again, were not like Earth colors. Overhead, she could see swarms of brightly colored birds or insects flying in dancing patterns across the sky.

"It's… beautiful," she said.

L'chong bowed. "Thank you. Trevelor is a hospitable planet."

They were all loaded into a bus-like ambulance, but unlike Earth ambulances, it had a ring of windows through which they could see their surroundings. The attendants fastened the stretchers into place and monitors began emitting a stream of data, none of which Abby could read. She hoped that the fact that no alarms were sounding was a good sign. Looking back through the windows, Abby noticed a vehicle emerging from the ship with several Cires onboard.

L'chong saw it too and smiled at Hrebec. "Once a warrior, always a warrior?"

"How did you know?" Hrebec demanded.

The medic shrugged. "As I said, we have treated many kinds of people here."

"Have you treated Cires before?"

L'chong gave him a considering look as the ambulance accelerated smoothly. "I suspect you are here because you are aware of that. However, I would never breach a patient's confidentiality."

"I see," Hrebec said grimly.

As they moved away from the landing area and into the city proper, Abby watched in fascination. The buildings were painted in an eye-catching display of bright colors that should have clashed but somehow managed to combine into a harmonious whole. The smaller ones, apparently residential, were topped with thatched roofs, and she had the sudden urge to giggle as she realized that they reminded her of birdhouses.

The ambulance pulled up in front of a long, low building that was painted in shades of pink. As Abby followed the stretchers inside, she just had time to notice that the building was surrounded by an abundance of flowering plants. Inside, a wide corridor wound past a number of rooms with gaily painted curtains covering the doorways. Some of the curtains were open, and she caught glimpses of a startling variety of species in addition to the Trevelorians. Her anxiety eased a little.

"Why are there so many different species here?" she whispered to Hrebec.

L'chong was just in front of them but he turned his head at her question. "We are a peaceful planet and, although we did not escape the Red Death, we were not as devastated as many planets. We have welcomed refugees from those troubled worlds."

"That was very generous of you," she said sincerely.

"It was to our benefit as well. It has helped to replace those we lost and we have gained much in knowledge and skills. Diversity is nature's way." He stopped outside a room, pushing aside a curtain of yellow and blue circles. "Miss Amber will go in here. Medic Mekoi, will you accompany her?"

"You're going to separate the girls?" Abby asked L'chong in a low voice.

"I think it is best. I have every reason to expect that she will have a normal labor and delivery. Miss Molly will require more specialized care." He saw her hesitation. "Do not fear. They will not be far apart."

She didn't like it, but he seemed to know what he was doing. TeShawna and Mekoi accompanied Amber inside, but Abby was relieved to see that Hrebec gestured for two of his men to remain as well. Biting her lip, she followed Molly's stretcher.

They passed through a set of glass doors into another section of the hospital. It was quieter here, with an air of hushed serenity that bore more resemblance to a church than to a medical ward. Even the colors were quieter, changing to soft pastels. L'chong led the way into a large room that looked out onto a small garden. Everything in the room was in soft shades of blue, and at first glance there was nothing to indicate that it was a hospital room. She watched in amazement as the stretcher somehow merged with the bed and the monitors floated up onto the walls. Even they seemed to resemble more of an abstract pattern of lights than the blinking, beeping units with which she was familiar.

"Now," L'chong said. "Where is the father?"

"Back on Earth."

"Was he involved with the pregnancy?"

"Ha," she said bitterly. "As soon as he realized that she was pregnant, he dumped her. At least he was thoughtful enough to bring her to me."

"I see. And the Cire?" He looked at Ribel, who was crouched over Molly, his tail still around her wrist.

"We suspect that they are mates," Hrebec said.

"Have they been together?"

"No," Abby said.

The Trevelorian made a disapproving noise and Abby felt compelled to explain. "She is very young— underage by our standards—and Captain Hrebec is returning us to Earth. It didn't seem wise to encourage them to spend time together."

"Hmm." L'chong frowned at Hrebec. "You did not trust your crew member to behave with honor?"

"I trust him. He would—he did—choose to take the honorable action and stay away from her."

L'chong shook his head. "A bond cannot be dismissed that easily. In this case, it appears to have caused damage to the female."

Guilt flooded Abby. "That was never my intention! We have nothing like a mating bond on Earth…"

"I'm sure you meant no harm," he assured her. "And Captain, I suspect that the tragic fate of Ciresia over the past generation has meant that much knowledge of the mating bond has been lost."

"So what do we do?" Abby asked.

"We will continue administering the supplements that Medic Mekoi started. They will give her body strength. I have also added something to slow her labor, but it will only be effective for a short period. When a child is ready to be born, they cannot be delayed for too long." His beaked nose twitched. "What I believe would help her most would be to allow the bond to flower between them."

"What?" Abby had to fight to keep her voice low. "Surely you aren't suggesting that he have sex with her? She isn't even conscious."

"Of course not. A physical joining is only one aspect of the bond." He observed her flaming cheeks. "Were you not aware of that?"

"Um, no." Hrebec's tail patted her hand comfortingly and she clasped it in her hand.

L'chong nodded approvingly. "Yes, like that. I propose that we surround her with his scent, his presence, and hope that she can use his strength to bolster her own."

"Will it be dangerous for Ribel?" Hrebec asked.

"It could be. It will, of course, be his decision." L'chong paused. "I'm not sure that it will be possible to separate them afterward, although there are some alternatives we can try."

"But... she's going back to Earth." Abby looked at the fragile figure in the bed, dwarfed by the mound of her stomach. "Is there anything else you can do?"

"I can try, but I will tell you this directly. I think this is the only chance to save her life."

"How could it have come to this? Why didn't I see what was happening?" At her despairing words, Hrebec pulled her closer.

L'chong made a sympathetic noise. "Do not blame yourself. Her body shows signs of long-standing weaknesses. That weakness may have been aggravated by recent events, but unless your planet has technology of which I am unaware, going into labor would always have put her in jeopardy."

She took a deep breath. "Do it. Do whatever you can to save her and the baby."

He nodded. "You have made a wise decision."

L'chong went to a small object in a niche on the wall that she had assumed was a sculpture and made some adjustments. The bed widened and lengthened. Ribel barely seemed to notice, his gaze focused on Molly's face, until the medic spoke to him.

"Ribel, this female needs your help. Will you assist her?"

"Of course. Anything."

"It could be dangerous," L'chong warned. "She is extremely weak and trying to helping her could drain you beyond your ability to recover."

Ribel finally looked at him, and Abby's heart ached at the despair on his young face. "I don't care. There would be no life for me if she died. Only the thought that she would be safe and happy on her planet has sustained me these past days."

L'chong nodded. "Then join her. Wrap yourself around her. She will need your strength."

Ribel climbed into the bed and tucked Molly carefully into his arms, his tail curving over her waist and hugging her close to him. Thin silvery ribbons appeared from the ceiling, floating down and weaving themselves around the young couple.

"They will provide additional nutrition," L'chong explained softly. "We will leave them now. I will monitor from outside the room, but I want them to be alone together as much as possible."

Abby left without protest, but as soon as they were outside, she stopped. "What about the labor?"

"I will postpone it as long as possible to give her time to strengthen, but I do not think it will be possible to wait more than another day, perhaps less. Do you wish to wait with her?"

"Yes, but..." She looked up at Hrebec. "What about the girls?"

"I can provide you with rooms," L'chong said. "We are equipped for family stays."

"Could we do that?" she asked Hrebec. "I know you have the ship to look after."

"The ship will be fine," he assured her. "I will get the girls and return."

As they walked towards Amber's room, Abby remembered TeShawna and Mekoi. "I hate to infringe upon your hospitality, but would you have another room? I think TeShawna would like to stay with her friend, and she has a child as well."

"Of course. We have plenty of room at this time." L'chong tilted his head in a very birdlike gesture. "May I ask how many children are on this ship?"

"Aside from my little girl, there are six infants. There are two other human females as well."

"Indeed." He bobbed his head thoughtfully.

"One of them is a Cire infant," Hrebec said grimly. "Purchased at this hospital."

"Purchased? Ah, I see. The Vedeckian who promised to find a Cire home for her." He shook his head. "I did not suspect him of ill intentions. He seemed genuinely concerned with the welfare of the child."

"I think he was," Abby said. Ignoring Hrebec's snort, she continued. "However, his... companions were not. They intended to sell the baby."

"How is she? Cire infants do not thrive without a family bond. We were in the middle of an outbreak of disease and I was not able to attend to the matter personally. That is one of the reasons I agreed to let her go."

"She has a family now," she said firmly, and Hrebec's tail wrapped around her arm.

"I see." Sharp little eyes darted between them. "As I said, we have plenty of room. Perhaps the other females and the infants would like to spend some time on the planet. And if you do bring them here, I would be happy to check the health of the infants." He nodded to Hrebec. "They are not needed, but you may bring your guards as well."

"Thank you for the offer," Abby said.

"You are most welcome. I have duties to attend to, but I will speak with you soon." He dipped his head, another gesture that accented his avian heritage, and walked away with his hopping gait.

"Do you think that would be all right?" she asked Hrebec. "To bring everyone here? If they want to come?"

"Would you like that?"

"I think it would be nice for everyone to have some fresh air. And this is really an amazing place."

"Then I will take care of it," he promised. Ignoring the fact that his men were watching, he pulled her closer. "I do not wish to leave you, my mate."

She didn't protest the term this time, despite her doubts for the future. Instead, she slid her hands up to his broad shoulder. "I don't want you to leave either, but you need to get our girls. I'll be fine."

"I know you will." He bent his head and kissed her until she was breathless, then rested his brow briefly against hers. "I will return."

"I'll be waiting." She watched him leave and then, ignoring the averted eyes of the guards, went to join Amber.

Mama and the Alien Warrior

Chapter Twenty-Seven

Hrebec took the flyer back to the ship, arriving just in time to feed Tiana. Lucie was unusually petulant, demanding her mama and unhappy with having to wait while he fed Tiana. She finally burst into a flood of tears. He only managed to console her by perching her on his other knee while he gave Tiana her bottle.

She sniffed but nestled closer and poked the end of the bottle. "I wants a bottle."

His chest ached at her unhappiness, and he kept his voice gentle. "You're a big girl now, Lucie. You don't need a bottle."

"I don't wanna be a big girl." Her lower lip was out.

"Yes, you do. That way you can help Mama."

"But Mama's not here."

"We'll see her soon," he promised. "And she's going to need all your hugs and kisses. She's worried about Molly."

"I likes to help," she admitted.

"I know you do." He found that truth to be bittersweet, that he knew her so well in such a short amount of time. "Can you help me now by picking out something for Tiana to wear?"

"I wants to stay here with you."

He wanted her to stay too, but he knew she spoke only of the moment. He wanted his girls with him always.

He ran his tail over Lucie's soft hair. "You can sit with me until she's done. Why don't you tell me what you did with Pravit?"

Happier now, she told him how she had "helped" the cook make the mid-shift meal.

It took much longer than he had anticipated to gather the females and the infants and the supplies, but they finally arrived at the medical facility. As he had expected, Jedan and Inzen had both chosen to accompany him. He had left Sedlit in charge, reassuring himself that the young officer's duties were minimal and comforted by knowing that Pravit was still on board. Pravit might not be an officer, but he had both experience and common sense, and he could be trusted to watch over the younger men.

He found Abigail standing in the corridor, and at the sight of her, he felt a surge of pleasure and relief. If this was what a short separation felt like, how could he bear it when she finally left him for Earth?

Lucie went flying up to Abigail, her voice echoing in the corridor. "Oh, Mama, I missed you!"

"I missed you too, baby," she said, swinging her up into her arms.

As Hrebec drew closer, he realized that her cheeks were wet. "Abigail, is something wrong?"

She sighed and leaned into him as his tail pulled her to his side. "No, these are happy tears. Amber just had a beautiful little girl."

"Another girl? Yay!" Lucie cheered, and they both laughed.

"You can be a big sister to her too," Abigail said.

"But not like Tiana. Tiana's ours."

"Yes, she is," Abigail said, looking at him rather than the infant strapped to his chest. His throat grew tight.

"Do you know where our room is located?" he asked.

"Yes, L'chong showed it to me earlier." She shot him a mischievous glance. "I think you'll like it."

The room turned out to be a spacious suite with a living area and two bedrooms separated by a bathroom. At the sight of the second bedroom, he understood her reference. Tonight, he would have his wish: he and Abigail, alone in a big bed.

"Look, Mama, my room's pink!" Lucie bounced with excitement. "And there's a tub. Do you think they have rubber duckies?"

Abigail choked back a laugh when he frowned at the unfamiliar term. "I don't think so, baby, but maybe we can find some bubbles. Did you take a nap today?"

"No. And I don't need one. I's a big girl."

"Even big girls need naps," Abigail said as she yawned.

"Why don't you stay here and rest with Lucie?" he asked. "I need to talk to L'chong."

"That's not a bad idea," she said with a longing look at the bed.

His shaft stiffened at the thought of her, rumpled and sleepy against the pink sheets, but he sternly suppressed it. "Do you want me to take Tiana?"

"No, I missed her too. Come here, sweetheart." She cuddled the baby close and Tiana smiled up at her, her tail wrapping around Abigail's wrist.

He left her turning down the bed while Lucie chattered away. Although he wanted to stay, he needed to find out if L'chong had any information about Tiana's parents. He found the medic in a spacious office overlooking the front lawn.

L'chong rose from his chair. "Ah, Captain Hrebec. I suspected you would come by. Will you have a seat?"

"I'd prefer to stand, thank you." He had no reason to distrust the medic and was in fact grateful for his assistance, yet the pieces didn't add up. "Why do you know so much about Cire physiology? Especially if you only had one brief encounter with a female who was passing through?"

The medic settled back into this seat. "Why do you wish to know?"

He paced to the window and back. "My government is searching desperately for Cire females. As I'm sure you know, they were all taken by the Red Death."

"Yes, I had heard that." His sharp little eyes studied Hrebec. "Is that all?"

"No." He finally collapsed into a chair. "I want to know if Tiana has a family."

"You wish to give her up?"

"No! By Granthar, no. She is ours. But I can't help wondering if there is a family somewhere that misses her. A grandparent, perhaps."

L'chong watched him carefully. "Would it make you feel better to know that she has no one else?"

"Better? No. But I would feel better about adopting her if I knew that I wasn't replacing another claim."

"Adopting? Will your government permit that?"

The thought had never crossed his mind, but now that L'chong mentioned it, he remembered the messages he had received, the emphasis on Tiana, not as a person, but as a symbol. As an experiment.

His hands curled into fists. "I would never allow them to take her from me."

"Even if it meant you could never return to Ciresia?"

A realization struck him like a blow. "I never intended to return." He'd never said it aloud before, but he could hear the truth in the words.

"I see." It was L'chong's turn to pace. He bobbed up from his chair and hopped around the room with his odd gait. "Can I trust you, Captain?"

"I am trusting you with the lives of the females in my care."

"That is true. Will you give me your word of honor that you will not reveal the information I'm about to give you?"

"I will not keep anything from my mate."

L'chong waved a dismissive hand. "Of course. That is understood." He folded himself into the chair next to Hrebec's. "There is a Cire colony here on Trevelor."

The news was not a complete surprise, given the conversation leading up to it. "With both male and female Cires?"

"Yes, although even here, the males vastly outnumber the females. That is why many of them have taken non-Cire mates."

"Successfully?" he asked eagerly. "They have been able to have children and build a family?"

L'chong frowned. "In some cases. In others, they have chosen to adopt a child left in distressed circumstances by the aftermath of the Red Death."

Hrebec gestured impatiently. "By birth or adoption, they are still a family. I know that better than anyone."

The revelation still filled him with hope. The Cire race might change, but it would not be lost. He found the thought much more satisfying than the desperate hope that the scientists back on Ciresia would succeed with their artificial wombs and their experiments.

"I'm glad to hear you say that," L'chong said.

"But what of Tiana's parents? Were they part of the colony?"

"No. That may have been their intention, but they were both too ill to leave the facility. I truly do not know where they came from, but I do know that they came here as a last resort. Her father had contracted an illness during their travels, and we were unable to save him."

"And her mother?"

"She, too, was in a weakened state. Without her mate?" His head dipped. "I was surprised she lasted long enough to give birth, but she held on long enough to see her daughter."

"Tiana inherited her strength. She survived until Abigail arrived to find her and nourish her."

"In other words, to bond with her?"

"Yes." The thought that had been tormenting him emerged. "What will happen after Abigail leaves?"

"She is leaving the two of you?" L'chong looked shocked. "I thought you were a family unit."

"We are, but it's complicated. Abigail thinks it would be best for her daughter and the other females to return to Earth."

"I see." His head bobbed. "Has the infant bonded with you?"

"Yes, I think so. I love her as a daughter."

"That is an excellent start. I will examine her tomorrow and see what progress she has made." He shook his head. "I find it hard to believe I was so wrong about the Vedeckian."

"You knew he was a Vedeckian," Hrebec couldn't help pointing out.

"Every member of a race is not the same." L'chong's voice was gently chiding. "You should know that."

"You're right. I do know that. And he has been quite helpful," he admitted reluctantly.

L'chong dipped his head in acknowledgment. When it rose again, he studied Hrebec's face for a long moment.

"What is it?" he growled, uncomfortable with the scrutiny.

"I am wondering how you will do without your mate and the other child you have claimed as yours."

Pain spiked in his chest but he refused to give in to it. "I will do as I must. Tiana will need me."

"Yes, perhaps you are strong enough to go on. I suspect you already know how difficult it will be. Have you considered asking your mate to stay?"

"Of course. But as I said, she has a responsibility to her females, and I have a responsibility to my ship and my crew."

"I see."

They sat in silence for a few minutes before Hrebec got up to leave. At the door, he turned back. "I would like to visit this colony."

L'chong smiled. "I suspected as much. I have already sent a message and asked them to allow you to visit. I should hear back tomorrow."

"Thank you."

With what seemed to be characteristic thoughtfulness, L'chong arranged for Hrebec's group to have dinner together in a small garden area. The crew members Hrebec had assigned to the hospital joined the small group of families. Elaina and Jedan were never more than a few feet away from each other, and Abby noticed that Mekoi was just as close to TeShawna. Inzen had taken over caring for Lily, and he watched both her and Angel like a proud grandfather. Abby was grateful that he also kept a watchful eye on Cassie, and the young girl seemed comfortable in his presence. Lucie couldn't be still, racing around on the grass, picking flowers, and talking to everyone with breathless speed.

"She'll sleep well tonight," Abby laughed, as she watched her daughter trying to do a cartwheel in the soft grass.

"Good. I have plans for you," Hrebec growled in her ear, the deep rumble causing an immediate ache between her legs. She squirmed in her seat.

"I can tell you like that idea," he murmured.

"Oh, I do." She squeezed his tail where it was wrapped around her waist. "And I'm not sore anymore."

It was his turn to shift uncomfortably, and she saw him surreptitiously adjust himself.

Abby was pleased that Amber was able to join them briefly, looking tired but happy with her new daughter in her arms.

"I'm going to call her Trevi," she said. "After this beautiful place."

"That's a good name," Lucie decided. "Almost as good as Tiana."

They all laughed, but Abby couldn't help but be conscious of the missing member of the group. L'chong said that Molly was improving, but he was still deeply concerned. He wanted to hold off as long as possible before removing the drug preventing her from going into labor.

The evening wound to a close as the sun set and tiny bugs with colorfully lit bodies danced through the air. Amber returned to her room and most of the babies settled down for the night. Lucie had finally given up on chasing the tiny insects and was climbing up on Hrebec's lap when a muffled gasp made Abby look up.

Kwaret stumbled into the garden, one of the Trevelorians supporting him. Blood streamed from a gash over one eye.

"The ship!" he gasped. "Commander Khaen has escaped."

Mama and the Alien Warrior

Chapter Twenty-Eight

Hrebec passed Lucie to Abby then strode over to Kwaret. Abby followed close behind, pausing only to leave the girls in Cassie's care.

"What happened?" Hrebec demanded.

"I don't know," Kwaret said. "I was in the med lab. Cuvar and I heard a cry and he rushed out to see what was happening. I followed him, but by the time I arrived, I saw Commander Khaen standing over his body. When I bent down to check his breathing, Khaen must have struck me. As soon as I regained consciousness, I came to find you. I'm afraid... afraid he'll come after the females or the infants."

L'chong rushed out, his crest disheveled. "Our security measures have been armed. But if there is a determined attack..."

"If they have any sense, they'll be more focused on escaping," Hrebec said grimly. "Inzen, take everyone back to our rooms and secure the space. Take Dornic and Maraq. Jedan, go with L'chong and find out about these security measures. Arrange for guards outside of Amber and Molly's rooms. We won't try and move them unless it's necessary."

Jedan and L'chong departed immediately, while Inzen began organizing people, babies, and supplies.

"Is there anything I can do?" Kwaret asked Hrebec diffidently.

"When you left the ship, did you see any of my men?"

Kwaret shook his head. "No, but I was in a hurry to leave in case they came back. Cuvar was no longer there when I regained consciousness."

"Would Khaen harm my men?" Abby could hear the

dread in Hrebec's voice.

"I don't know." Kwaret twisted his hands. "There would be little profit in it and that is his usual motivation—but he is resentful that you took his ship."

"His ship..." Hrebec frowned. "Do you think he would try and take the *Defiance*?"

"Could he fly it?" Abby asked.

"Not without an authorization code, and no one on board has the code. He may be planning on trying to force the code from me when I return."

Abby grasped his arm. "Then don't go back."

"I have to go back. My men are there. In addition, that ship could do a lot of damage if he can override the security."

Every instinct urged her to beg him to remain, but she knew that he couldn't. "At least promise me you'll be careful." Despite her best efforts, her voice trembled.

"I will." He swept her into a hard but all too brief kiss. "I love you, Abigail."

"I love you too. Hurry back to me."

When he turned to leave, he stopped for a moment to address the Vedeckian. "Thank you, Kwaret. I appreciate your warning. Will you stay and help protect my family?"

"I would be honored." Kwaret bowed and Hrebec returned the gesture before gathering the rest of his men and leaving on the run.

Abby fought back her tears and instead went to help Inzen.

The night passed with an agonizing slowness. They had managed to find room for everyone in the suite thanks to some additional bedding from L'chong. She and the girls had taken the smaller bedroom, and thankfully the girls had gone to sleep without any protests.

A hint of grey had begun to touch the horizon before Abby heard a brief conversation in the living area, then a tall figure filled the doorway.

"Hrebec?" she whispered.

"Yes."

As he moved across the room, she noticed something odd about his silhouette. "What's wrong with your arm?"

"Just a superficial wound," he said, sliding into the bed next to her. "It has already been attended to."

With a relieved sigh, she nestled against the comfort of his big warm body, letting his scent surround her. His tail settled into its familiar position around her waist.

"What happened?" she asked at last.

"Khaen is dead, along with the other two Vedeckians." He sighed. "They had prepared an ambush, but since we had been warned, it was not successful."

"And your crew?"

"Most of them were in the brig."

She could hear the pain in his voice and was almost afraid to ask. "Most?"

"Connep was guarding them. He was killed in the escape. Cuvar is seriously wounded, but L'chong thinks he'll recover."

"I'm so sorry," she said, tightening her arms around him. "What about Pravit?"

"He's a clever old warrior. When he realized what was happening, he hid in one of the supply bins. Then when he heard us attacking, he hit them from behind."

She stroked his chest. "I know it's terrible to lose anyone, but I'm glad that no one else was killed."

"As am I." He grunted.

"What's wrong? Did I hurt you?"

"No, my flower. Lucie kicked me." He sighed. "So much for being alone in bed."

"It will happen one day."

"Will it?" His voice sounded tired and sad, and she had to fight back the lump in her own throat. "I don't want to lose you, Abigail."

"I don't want to lose you either, but what are we going to do? Lucie needs a home, an education, a future. And the other girls need me too."

"I know. And I have my crew to consider."

There was nothing else to be said. All she could do was wrap herself around him and hope that their remaining time together would last as long as possible.

The next morning, everyone seemed equally depressed despite Hrebec's success in reclaiming the ship. Hrebec fed Tiana before disappearing on some mysterious errand, which upset Lucie. Abby wasn't thrilled about it either, even though she knew he didn't owe her an explanation. Elaina and Jedan seemed unusually strained and tense with each other, while Cassie had wrapped herself in her old surly attitude. TeShawna snapped at Mekoi to the point where he bowed gravely and left.

When the girl immediately burst into tears, Abby led her into the bedroom. "What's the matter, TeShawna?"

"Nothing," she said defiantly, then her face crumpled again when Abby simply looked at her. "It's just..." Abby waited patiently for her to continue. "It's just that yesterday, when Amber had her baby, Mekoi was so wonderful. Calm and patient and... smart as a whip, you know?"

"Yes, he's a good doctor."

"And... and I want *that*. I wanna be a doctor," she burst out at last.

"TeShawna, that's wonderful. I think you'd make a great doctor."

"Yeah, right," she sneered. "I ain't nothing but a girl from the streets. I don't even have my GED."

"You were working on it. You're very close."

TeShawna didn't respond and Abby didn't push the issue. She suspected that there was more behind the girl's outburst than career dreams.

"Mekoi thought I could do it too," TeShawna said finally. "He was talking about the training I would need and how he could help me with Vanessa and with studying. We *forgot*."

"Forgot?"

"Forgot that he wouldn't be with me—with us." Dark eyes filled with tears again. "I don't wanna leave him."

Abby's heart ached. "Don't you want to go home?"

TeShawna scoffed. "What home? Staying with you's the only home that ever meant anything to me. Do we have to go back?"

"You don't think you'd be better off back on Earth than living in an alien spaceship?" She tried for a light tone, but the words rang hollow in her own ears. Wouldn't *she* rather be with Hrebec than back on Earth?

"No," TeShawna said baldly. She pursed her lips and a hint of her usual brashness appeared. "Maybe I'll decide to stay."

The words echoed in Abby's head. "You would really do that?"

"I don't know. I don't wanna be the only human, but... I don't wanna leave Mekoi either."

"Don't decide just yet, okay? Let me talk to Hrebec."

"Yeah, all right." Her defiant lower lip trembled. "Mekoi probably don't want me now, anyway."

"I sincerely doubt that. Why don't you go find him? I'll watch Vanessa."

"I don't like chasing after no man."

Abby patted her hand. "In this case, I think you owe him an apology, don't you?"

"Yeah, I reckon." A smile brightened her face for the first time that day. "I do like to kiss and make up."

"Well, go on then," Abby said with a laugh.

After that conversation, she wasn't really surprised when Elaina sought her out a short time later. She was much more direct than TeShawna had been.

"Jedan wants us to stay with him—and I want to stay," she said.

"What are the two of you going to do? Live on the ship? Bring up the babies there?"

"Maybe. At least for a while. But Jedan was thinkin' of settling down somewhere. Maybe buyin' a farm."

"A farm?"

"Yeah. What's wrong with that?" Elaina's lips twisted into a reminiscent smile. "I started off on one. It wasn't until times got hard and we had to sell and move to the city that things got bad with my dad. He wasn't happy anymore. That's when he started drinking."

"Aren't you concerned about being the only human out here?"

"Nah, not as long as I have Jedan, Mikie, and Ginger." She hesitated. "I do worry about the kids some, but it will be all they ever know, so I think they'll be fine."

"Has Jedan talked to Hrebec?"

"Not yet. I wanted to talk to you first. Do you think I'm doin' the right thing?"

"To be perfectly honest, I don't know," Abby said slowly. "I understand why you want to stay, but you have to think of the future as well."

Before she could continue, Cassie came rushing in. "Molly's in labor!"

Chapter Twenty-Nine

A fter a quick apology to Elaina and an assurance from Cassie that they'd take care of the girls, Abby went running.

When she arrived, the change in Molly's appearance shocked her. No longer pale and drawn, delicate color flushed her cheeks. The bed had been rearranged into a type of birthing chair and she was sitting up on her own. Ribel, on the other hand, looked like he'd lost twenty pounds overnight, but his voice was calm and certain as he urged Molly to breathe. Abby took Molly's other hand, and the girl squeezed it.

Molly glanced up at her. "I'm glad you're here."

"I'm glad I am too. Now, let's get this baby born."

"Fine with me," Molly said, clutching her hand as another contraction rolled through her.

Her labor seemed to last forever, although Abby knew that was just an illusion. Molly grew paler, while Ribel looked like only sheer force of will kept him going, although his voice never faltered. At long last, there was a gasping cry, and Molly's daughter was born. Ribel took one look at her before he collapsed.

"Ribel!" Molly cried.

L'chong had the bed extended once again. Once Ribel was lying next to Molly again, more silver ribbons wrapped around his wrists and ankles.

"He'll be fine," the medic assured them. "But he will need to rest for some time. As will you."

"But I have to take care of my daughter. Isn't she beautiful, Miss Abby?"

"Gorgeous, honey," Abby assured her. "And we'll

help with her, just like we have with all of the others. What are you going to call her?"

"I thought maybe Riba. I think Ribel would like that."

"I'm sure he would."

Abby helped Molly nurse Riba, slipping away when mother and child drifted into an exhausted sleep. A Trevelorian nurse stayed to watch over them while L'chong accompanied her out of the room.

"Is a mating bond always like that?" she asked. "It was like she actually drained him."

"No," he said. "Naturally, each partner draws strength from each other, but not to that extent. I encouraged the transfer of energy, but he also urged it on. As I warned you, they are more deeply bound now than ever before."

"She isn't going to want to leave him, is she?"

"No." He sighed. "But then again, I suspect she never did."

"She's so young…"

"Yes, but she will get older. As do we all."

Abby smiled ruefully at L'chong, and they parted ways, but as she returned to their suite, his words echoed in her thoughts. She wasn't getting any younger, and for the first time in her life, she felt truly happy. Three of her girls already wanted to stay with the Cires—although where they would stay was still up for debate. Would they need her more than the other two? But she couldn't just send them back to Earth without her.

When she returned to the room, everyone had left except Cassie and Inzen.

"Lucie had lunch and now she's taking a nap," Cassie said. "I wrapped Tiana in some of your clothes and managed to get her to take a bottle as well, although she wasn't happy about it."

Abby winced guiltily. "Hrebec isn't back? Since no one brought Tiana to me, I thought he must have taken care of her."

"Nah, he's not back. I would have brought her to you if I couldn't get her to take the bottle. How's Molly?"

"She and the baby are fine. They were sleeping peacefully when I left."

"And young Ribel?" Inzen asked.

"Drained. Whatever L'chong did seemed to take his strength and pass it on to Molly. I hope he's going to be okay."

"I'm sure he will be fine," Inzen said, "but he would have willingly made any sacrifice to assist his mate."

Cassie looked at him, then took a deep breath. "Miss Abby, TeShawna told me that she's thinking about staying. I am too."

"You?" Abby stared at her in shock. She hadn't expected this from the practical Cassie. Unless… "You mean… you and Inzen are mates?"

"No," they both said at the same time.

"Cassie is like a daughter to me," Inzen assured her. "But as a father, I am concerned for her safety and her happiness. She has not been treated well on this Earth of yours."

She couldn't argue with that. "And this is what you want, Cassie?"

"Yes." The girl's face softened. "I feel—I feel like I've found a family, and I don't want to lose that."

Abby sighed. "I understand. That's four of you."

"Four?"

"Elaina intends to stay with Jedan, and while I

haven't discussed it with Molly, I'm quite certain she won't want to leave Ribel."

"We could talk Amber into staying," Cassie said eagerly.

"No. I don't want you to even try. This has to be her decision."

"And what about you, Abigail?" Inzen asked. "Do you want to stay?"

"I have to think about Lucie," she said, knowing she was avoiding the question.

"You come from a place that has produced five pregnant females without family support. Is that what you want for your daughter?"

"Not everyone ends up in that position," she protested, even though over the past four years, she had seen all too much of it.

He inclined his head. "You would know, of course."

"Are you proposing that everyone stay on the ship?" she asked. "That doesn't seem fair to the babies or the girls."

"You are correct." Inzen hesitated. "I haven't yet discussed this with Hrebec, but—"

"Discussed what?" Hrebec asked from the doorway.

"My intention to resign," Inzen finished calmly.

Chapter Thirty

W hen Hrebec awoke the morning after the battle, he found himself obsessing about the Cire colony that L'chong had revealed. He needed to see for himself what type of society they had developed. After feeding Tiana, he went to speak to L'chong. He didn't tell Abigail where he was going for reasons he didn't want to examine too closely. The efficient medic had already arranged for transportation, and a small personal flyer with the route programmed into its system awaited him.

As he flew towards his destination, he admired the landscape. He passed over several small cities, but the planet was predominantly rural with farms interspersed with large natural areas. The natural beauty was a welcome change from both Ciresia's devastation and the familiar but confined surroundings on the *Defiance*.

The flyer finally landed in a small clearing at the top of a hill. From here, he could look down at the village. A large central market square was surrounded by a cluster of buildings that followed the Trevelorian tradition of bright colors and thatched roofs. None of the buildings were large, and he saw no signs of industry. Fields stretched from the village down to the river and he could see people working in them. The path leading down from the landing site was surrounded by orchards.

Despite the peaceful, idyllic scene, his heart sank. While he hadn't allowed himself to consciously consider the matter, he had thought that perhaps this could be a solution for himself and Abigail. While it was no doubt attractive, how could he ask her to live in a remote village under such primitive conditions? She had mentioned Lucie's education several times, and he doubted that the opportunities available here would rise beyond a tiny school and an inexperienced teacher.

At the bottom of the hill, he was met by an older Cire, perhaps his father's age, who studied him closely. "Hrebec? Son of Charen?"

Hrebec stared at him. "How did you know?"

"You resemble him closely." He extended his hand, and Hrebec automatically clasped his wrist briefly before the other man continued. "I am Dirigen. You were too young to remember, but I was friends with your parents. I'm sorry about your mother. She was a lovely woman. When she died, it triggered my own decision to leave. I could see the way the authorities were heading, and I wanted out before it was too late." He turned to lead the way deeper into the village. "What brings you here? L'chong has assured me that you do not intend to report on our existence to Ciresia."

"No, I won't do that."

As they reached the market square, he looked around in amazement. There were a number of Cires present, mostly male, but he saw two females. At least four other species mingled with the crowd. Several children were darting around, all bearing signs of mixed heritage.

Dirigen laughed. "The High Council would most definitely not approve." He waved a hand, and Hrebec realized that he was referring to the number of different species in the small village.

"Have you been here ever since you left Ciresia?" he asked.

"No. We traveled for several years, tried a stint on Darchan, and finally ended up here."

Dirigen seemed satisfied, but Hrebec had his doubts. "Isn't it a very... simple life? Our ancestors lived like this."

"It may appear that way, but I assure you we are not missing any modern conveniences. Except for indoor sanitary facilities, of course." Dirigen burst into laughter at Hrebec's appalled silence. "You should see your face. I promise you that our sanitary systems are quite up to date."

A reluctant grin crossed Hrebec's face. "I am relieved to know that."

"I'm sure you are. But again, why are you here?"

Hrebec sighed. "It's a long story."

"Then come inside. We'll have a drink while you tell me."

Dirigen led the way through a small but comfortable house. Hrebec caught enough of a glimpse of both the kitchen and bathroom areas to realize that they were quite modern. They ended up on a back porch overlooking the river. Dirigen poured them each a glass of wine while Hrebec told his tale.

"A female Cire infant." Dirigen said, when Hrebec was finished. "I wonder why L'chong did not send her to us." His brow ridges crinkled. "Is that why you're here? To see if we'll take her?"

"No," he said immediately. "She's ours."

Dirigen's lips quirked. "Ours?"

"She is the daughter of my mate and myself."

"Your human mate," Dirigen said thoughtfully.

The sound of laughter floated over to their position and Hrebec turned to see a couple walking up the path from the river. The man was Cire and the female was Trevelorian, but they were walking hand in hand, his tail wrapped protectively around her feathered shoulders, and they were quite obviously in love.

"Do you have a problem with humans?" he asked, turning back to Dirigen.

"How could I? I've never met one. I was referring more to the fact that you said she wished to return to her planet."

Hrebec looked at the other man and admitted, "I thought—I thought that perhaps this would be an alternative. But how can I ask her to live in a place like this when she is accustomed to a different lifestyle? Her planet may not have space flight, but their technology seems relatively sophisticated."

Dirigen shrugged. "We have all the technology we need. We travel regularly to Wiang and are quite aware of what is happening in the Confederation."

"She is also concerned about the education of our daughters."

"My granddaughter just graduated from the university in Wiang." Dirigen's eyes narrowed. "But these are simply excuses. The question is—will you let her go back to her planet?"

"I cannot stop her," he said, his chest aching as he spoke.

"Perhaps not. But you can decide what you are willing to give up to have her stay."

"Everything." There was no hesitation in his response. The thought of his ship and his crew flitted through his mind, but they were insignificant compared to Abigail and his family.

"Then you have your answer. Offer her everything you have, and hope that it is enough."

"What if it's not?"

"What if it is? My mate was willing to give up Ciresia and travel with me on an unknown quest. You cannot know unless you ask."

Hrebec bowed his head in acknowledgment and

Dirigen let the subject drop. They finished their wine, and then the older man gave him a tour of the village. There was a larger variety of commerce than he had anticipated, and he found himself wondering where he could fit in. At least part of the answer came when they entered a building and found an elderly Trevelorian making furniture.

"These are beautiful," Hrebec said, noticing the way the lines of each piece brought out the subtle colors in the wood.

Dirigen laughed. "I'm not surprised you appreciate them. Your father was a talented furniture maker at one time."

"He was? I only remember him rushing off to the lab every morning."

"That was after your mother died. He was so determined to prevent others from suffering her fate. Did he get rid of everything he made?"

"No," he said slowly, remembering some of the beautiful pieces that had graced his home up until the time they had moved because the labs were consolidated. The desk currently on his ship was the only one of them to survive the move.

Fascinated, he wandered over to the owner and was soon deeply engrossed in conversation. Dirigen eventually had to politely, but firmly, suggest that they be on their way. Their last stop was the school. Rather than one massive building, the school was comprised of small pods connected by a trellised loggia. Dirigen introduced him to the principal, a no-nonsense Trevelorian with a kind face and an air of competency. She willingly discussed the curriculum and he found himself reluctantly impressed.

Finally, Dirigen walked with him back to the flyer. "So what do you think?"

"I believe that I misjudged the village."

The other man laughed. "I agree, and I hope you will consider joining us. You would be most welcome. But Hrebec, this isn't the only solution. No matter what you were taught on Ciresia, you do not have to be surrounded by other Cires. If your mate would prefer city living, stay in the city. If she doesn't like Trevelor, find another planet. In the end, what really matters is that she is with you."

Dirigen's parting words had stayed with him during the flight home. Anxious to discuss them with Abigail, he didn't expect to walk in and hear his chief engineer announcing his retirement.

Chapter Thirty-One

"What did you say?" Hrebec asked as Inzen bowed his head.

"I said that I intend to resign. Cassie does not wish to return to Earth, and I intend to build a family with her."

Shocked, he darted his gaze between the pair. "You are mates?"

Inzen shook his head. "No, although everyone seems to be making that assumption. I feel as a father would."

"You haven't heard the rest of it," Abigail said dryly. "Elaina, TeShawna, and Molly don't want to return either. We were just discussing possible alternatives to having them spend the rest of their lives on the ship."

"I may have one," he said slowly. "Does that mean that you would stay also?"

Abigail bit her lip, but before she could respond, Inzen cleared his throat. "We will leave you to discuss this matter." He and Cassie picked up the two infants and left.

"Well, Abigail?"

"I want to stay with you. But I have a responsibility to Lucie—and to Amber. And you said you had a responsibility to your ship and your crew."

"I have been considering that." For his entire homeward flight. "I believe that some of my crew would choose to stay here."

"Here? On Trevelor?"

"Yes. I'll come back to that. But I know that not all of them want to stay. They are young, anxious for adventure, and I did make a commitment to the

Confederation."

Her face fell. "I see."

"No, you don't. I have spent all this time thinking that I was the only one who could handle the responsibility, but that was foolish." He shook his head. "I was behaving as badly as the High Council, thinking of it as only a Cire ship that required a Cire captain. If I can find a good captain —of any species—I will donate the ship. My men may choose to stay here or to go with the new captain."

"But it's your ship..."

"It's not as important to me as you are, Abigail," he said firmly. "I know you don't want to raise the girls onboard."

"No, but I didn't want you to give it up. What's this alternative you mentioned?"

"I went on a journey this morning." He told her about the village, watching her face carefully. To his relief, she seemed excited and was not as dismissive of the rural life as he had feared.

"As long as they have a good school, I love the idea of living somewhere peaceful." She got up and began pacing the room.

"It's true I've always lived in the city, but I could adapt to country life. And this planet is beautiful." Her footsteps slowed. "But I can't forget Amber, Hrebec. If she wants to return to Earth, I have to go with her and make arrangements for her. It could take some time, especially with such a new baby. Would you—could you wait for me?"

"I would wait for you forever, my mate," he said sincerely.

"And you could come back for me?"

"Of course." How could she doubt it? Despite the fact that it was strictly prohibited, he would never let a mere law keep him from his mate. "I will maintain ownership of the *Defiance* until you can return."

"I can't believe we can actually be together."

Her eyes filled with tears but then she flew across the room and kissed him frantically. He met her mouth with equal urgency, pulling her closer, hands and tail roaming over her body. He had just worked his way inside her top, when a small voice came from across the room.

"Mama, you's kissing Papa again—I mean Leonardo," she added sadly.

Abigail dashed the tears from her cheeks and smiled at their daughter. "Come here, Lucie."

She came eagerly, climbing up between them and winding an arm around each neck.

"Remember how I said we had to go home?" Abigail asked gently.

Lucie's face fell, her lip poking out. "Yeah. I don't wants to."

"How about after we go home for a little while, we come back to stay with Hrebec?"

"Forever?" Lucie's eyes widened.

"Yes, forever," he said.

Her eyes flew to his. "And you's be my Papa for real?"

"Yes, little one."

"Yay! That would be the best thing ever. Better than… better than ice cream!"

He laughed and drew his family close, his own eyes stinging.

Abby pulled away from their happy huddle long enough to get Tiana from her bassinet.

"You'll always be my daughter now," she whispered

to the baby. Tiana smiled up at her and wrapped her tail around Abby's wrist, as if she understood Abby's words. Abby's eyes filled with tears again and she hugged her close. "That's my girl."

They joined Hrebec and Lucie on the couch, where her daughter was peppering him with eager questions about the village. Abby could see that she had already forgotten the part about returning to Earth first. Deciding that it would be best to find out where they stood as soon as possible, she excused herself and went to visit Amber. The girl still looked tired but radiantly happy. Abby admired Trevi, then hesitated, not quite sure how to broach the subject.

"Let me guess," Amber said after Abby's silence stretched out. "You want to talk to me about returning to Earth."

"How did you know?"

"You think TeShawna can keep her mouth shut?"

"Amber, I want you to understand that there's absolutely no pressure on you to stay here. If you want to return, I'll go with you and remain until you're in a place where you feel comfortable."

"And then what? Are you going to stay on Earth?"

She hesitated for a fraction of second before shaking her head. "No. We're coming back to be with Hrebec and Tiana."

"Then you don't need to go back there just for me."

"I want to make sure you understand that you don't have to stay here if you don't want to."

Amber plucked at Trevi's blanket and then looked at Abby. "Do you know how I ended up with you?"

"No." Amber was her newest girl and they hadn't talked much about her history. Abby only knew that the baby's father had died.

"I'm not like the other girls—I actually had a happy childhood. My mom and dad were great. But then when I was thirteen, they were killed in a car accident. I ended up living with my mom's aunt. I'd only met her once or twice before." She shrugged. "She wasn't bad. She just didn't care that much. Oh, if I stayed out too late, she'd tell me not to do it again, but then she'd forget all about it. I did a lot of stupid things trying to get her attention, but it never really worked. Then I met Danny." Her mouth curved in a reminiscent smile. "I really loved him and he loved me, too. We started making plans to get married as soon as I graduated."

She grew silent, looking off into the past, before she continued. "He died. Just happened to be in a convenience store when some asshole with a gun decided to rob it and shoot up the place. Two weeks later, I found out I was pregnant. I wanted the baby, so I didn't tell anyone. I tried to hide it and did a pretty good job. I was eight months along before my aunt saw me changing one day and realized that I wasn't just getting fat. All that time trying to get her attention? Well, I had it then."

"What happened?" Abby asked, her heart already breaking.

"She said it was bad enough having to take care of one kid that wasn't hers—she wasn't about to take on two. Dragged me to the doctor and got so pissed when she found out it was too late for an abortion. That's when she dropped me off at your door."

"I'm so sorry, Amber."

"Not your fault. But my point is I don't have a family on Earth—I have one here with you and the girls. Please don't make me leave."

"I would never do that." Unable to restrain her tears, Abby reached over and hugged the girl. Amber hugged her back just as tightly before finally giving a watery sniffle.

"So what's the deal? Are we going to become permanent residents on the ship?"

When Amber handed her a tissue, Abby blew her nose and smiled. "I think we have a better plan."

Chapter Thirty-Two

I t wasn't until Abby left Amber's room that the realization finally hit her. They were going to stay with Hrebec. When she practically skipped back into their rooms, he took one look at her face and greeted her with a matching smile.

"You're staying?" he asked.

She beamed at him. "We're staying."

He laughed and whirled her around while Lucie giggled and Tiana grinned toothlessly.

The rest of the day disappeared in a blur of plans and schedules. It wasn't until later that night that they were finally alone together. She waited in silent anticipation as he solemnly locked the doors to the living areas and to the connecting bathroom.

"You know that doesn't mean they won't need us, right?" she asked. "It's part of the joys of parenthood."

"And I wouldn't trade it for all the credits in the galaxy," he said. "But I would appreciate just one night alone with my beautiful mate and a big bed."

"Just one?" she asked breathlessly as he stripped off his clothes and prowled towards her, tail lashing. Every inch of that big muscled body was hers now, and she shivered with anticipation.

"I hope for many." He knelt at the bottom of the bed. "But I'll start with one."

With startling speed, he pulled her hips up and buried his face between her legs, licking every inch as if he couldn't get enough of her. She was already wet but he demanded more, teasing her clit, probing her entrances, overwhelming her with sensation, and sending her soaring into a rapid climax.

"That's better," he growled. "I have missed this delicious cunt."

"I've missed you too."

He worked his way up her body, slower this time, spending a long time on her breasts, teasing the sensitive peaks until they were aching and distended and she was tugging at his shoulders. When he finally left them and kissed her, she could taste herself on his tongue, mingling with his own delicious taste.

His tail had been teasing her clit as he kissed her and now it dipped lower, working its way into her pussy. She moaned and he raised his head.

"Are you still sore?" he asked.

"Oh, no. That feels amazing."

"Good." His tail slid deeper, vibrating rapidly.

"You're going to make me come again," she warned.

"Good," he repeated, his tail thrusting in and out as she clutched at him.

"I want you inside me this time." A wicked thought struck her. "I have an idea."

He grinned down at her. "I like your ideas, my mate."

"Let me turn over."

He drew back with a puzzled expression. "I don't understand. How can I—"

He choked on his words as she flipped over and wiggled her butt at him. His big hands covered her cheeks, squeezing gently, and his scent thickened, the musky notes dominating.

"This is most enticing," he said in a husky voice as he traced her folds with his cock, the texture firing her senses. Her breath caught as he rubbed back and forth against her clit.

"Inside me," she gasped.

"As you wish, my mate."

Then the broad head was at her entrance. Despite their last encounter, it was still a tight fit and he had to keep pressing until her entrance finally loosened enough for him to enter.

"This is even better than I remembered," he murmured as he continued to work his way into her pussy.

His tail was at her clit, teasing the swollen nub and distracting her from the immense stretch as her body softened. When he was finally embedded, he leaned forward, his body shaking.

"I will not last long," he warned.

In response, she tightened her pussy as much as she could around his massive cock. He shuddered and began thrusting, his tail working her clit faster, as the pleasure began building. He groaned and plunged deeper, and she felt him expanding, stretching her body open as he came in a long, shuddering wave. Her body quivered, right on the edge of climax, and breathed a protest as his tail left her clit, but his finger replaced it, stroking slowly, too slowly across the needy flesh.

"Hrebec, please..."

"I have an idea of my own," he whispered.

She felt his tail probing at her bottom hole. "What
—"

The tip slipped inside, adding impossibly to the fullness, and she could feel each nub rubbing across her sensitive tissues as his finger circled, harder now, and sparks of light shot across her vision as she came in a burst of almost painful pleasure.

When she finally stopped shaking, Hrebec rolled them to one side, still deeply embedded in her body, and cupped her breast.

"I am lucky to have such a creative mate," he murmured.

"You were pretty creative there yourself."

"Did you enjoy it?"

"You know I did."

"Good. Because I'm about to get creative again."

Abby sighed happily.

A considerable time later, Hrebec withdrew carefully from Abigail's limp body and unlocked the bathroom so that he could cleanse her. As soon as he was done, he gathered her close. She snuggled against him and stroked his chest.

"I'm so glad we found each other," she whispered.

"Granthar has smiled on us," he agreed.

"Mm." She wiggled a little, stopping only when his body responded. "Hrebec, you're hard again. I thought that after you knotted, you didn't remain hard."

"I didn't remain hard," he corrected her. "I am hard again."

She rolled over and arched her back so that the tips of her luscious breasts rubbed against his chest. "Well, in that case, maybe we should take—"

They both heard the whimper from the monitor.

Hrebec laughed. "I suppose I should be grateful she waited this long." He stood up and pulled on his sleep pants, tossing Abigail his shirt. "I'll go get her."

As he went to get his daughter, he realized there was one last thing he would need to do to separate himself from his old world.

The next morning, he arranged to use L'chong's conference room to send a message to Ciresia. Joining him in the conference room were the shipmates who were choosing this new life with him. His family was there as well, with Lucie warned to be silent.

He stood alone on one side of the room so that his would be the only figure visible in the screen.

After a brief pause, the weathered features of Councilman Okaza appeared. "Well, Captain Hrebec? Did you find any other Cire females?"

Everyone in the room held their breath.

"No," Hrebec said finally. "It appears that the female who gave birth came from one of the ships that stopped here, but so far we haven't found any records to indicate which one."

Okaza sighed. "That is disappointing, but not surprising. It was too much to hope that another female would survive. This makes it even more imperative that you bring the infant female to us as soon as possible."

This was the difficult part. "Would that still be true if she wasn't of pure Ciresian blood?"

"What?" Okaza recoiled. "I thought her mother was Cire. Her father must have been also. We cannot mate with other races."

"We don't know that for sure," he pointed out. "We have not made an effort to confirm whether or not it is true."

"And we will not. We are trying to save our race, not create a new race of half-breeds." Okaza's face wrinkled with distaste. "Are you sure that the infant is not a true Cire?"

"I'm sure that her mother is—was—not actually Cire."

"How disappointing." Okaza sighed. "Perhaps it

would be best if you did not bring her back to Ciresia. I do not want any of these young fools getting the wrong idea."

"Yes, Okaza." After a brief pause, he continued. "However, I still feel a responsibility for the infant. Under the circumstances, I will not be returning either."

Okaza raised an eye ridge. "Since you abandoned your position at the Reproduction Laboratory to go on this misguided adventure in the first place, I'm not surprised. I shudder to think what your father would have said."

"I don't think he would be surprised," Hrebec said slowly, looking around the room at his mate and his girls, at his companions.

"Perhaps not," Okaza acknowledged. "Your efforts have been most helpful and so I wish you well, Hrebec."

"Thank you."

He disconnected the call and smiled as he took another look around. His old life was behind him now and he felt not an ounce of regret. His future awaited.

Epilogue

Two years later

"Mama, fireworks!" Lucie burst into the room just as Abby was putting the baby to sleep.

As usual, Tiana was right behind her, but even at two years old, she was still a quiet and observant child. Abby often wondered how much her first traumatic months had influenced her, but all that really mattered was that she was now safe and happy.

"Shh, Lucie. Let me get your brother asleep first."

"But doesn't Leo want to see the fireworks?"

It was perhaps inevitable that when Abby gave birth to a boy, Lucie had insisted that he should be called Leonardo. Since Hrebec was equally as enthusiastic, Abby didn't attempt to argue.

"He's just a baby, sweetie."

Lucie pouted. "But I want him to see."

"Perhaps next year, when he's older," Hrebec said firmly as he followed the girls into the room. "I think Mama's glad he's sleeping right now."

She laughed and nodded. Leo was cutting his first tooth, and he'd kept both of them up most of the previous night. Hrebec had been at her side the whole time, just as he always was whenever she needed him. She gave his tall, broad figure an appreciative look, her heart still beating a little faster in his presence.

"Come on, girls. Let your mama put your brother to bed so she can come watch with us."

"Yes, Papa," they chorused.

Both of them stopped to plant a kiss on Leo's cheek

before they followed Hrebec. Big, dark eyes, so much like his father's, blinked up at them, his mouth forming a sleepy grin. He was almost the spitting image of Hrebec, only the pale gold of his skin indicating his human heritage.

When they had decided to try for a baby, she hadn't really expected to get pregnant, but she had been thrilled when it happened. Hrebec was just as excited. Once Leo was born, they had debated telling the High Council, but in the end decided against it. Ciresia was still fixated on producing "pure" Cire children. At least their suggestions had helped and the survival rate was significantly higher.

Sitting back in the rocking chair, she hummed and rocked until Leo's eyes closed again, then placed him in the wooden crib handed down from Tiana. It had been one of Hrebec's first projects and the sides were not completely even, but she loved it and had firmly refused his offer to make a new one. She turned on the communication bracelet she still used as a baby monitor and went to join her family.

They were all gathered on the front veranda, Lucie and Tiana on either side of Hrebec on the wide wooden bench. Abby scooped up Tiana so that she could sit next to Hrebec. Her daughter snuggled down in her arms, turning her head to breathe in Abby's scent as she wrapped her tail around Abby's wrist.

"Will everyone be here tomorrow, Mama?" Lucie asked.

"Yes, sweetie. They're all coming to celebrate the new baby."

Although the presence of the Cire colony had tipped the decision to stay on Trevelor, not everyone had actually moved to the village. TeShawna and Mekoi had decided to remain in Wiang so TeShawna could study medicine while he worked at the medical facility. Cassie had also decided to stay and, with Inzen's encouragement, had opened a small dress shop that was doing remarkably well. The four of them shared the house over the shop, and Inzen had happily taken on a large part of the childcare for all three babies.

Elaina and Jedan, of course, had been happy to move to the village and purchase the farm they had dreamed about. Molly and Ribel had lived with them for the first year, at which point Molly had come to Abby and told her quite firmly that they were not going to wait any longer before becoming mates in every sense. Abby couldn't argue. The young couple had shown their devotion to each other and their daughter.

Amber and her daughter had spent the first six months living with Abby and Hrebec in the room that was now Leo's. Part of her time had been spent helping out in the village school and she had ended up falling in love with one of the teachers, a tall Trevelorian male with an impressive jade green crest. They had just given birth to their first child and both the fireworks tonight and the celebration tomorrow were in honor of the birth.

There was a trail of light down by the river, then a brilliant burst of color exploded overhead. Unlike Earth fireworks, there was no following boom, just a distant flutter.

"Ooh, aah," Abby said.

"What's that, Mama?" Lucie asked.

"It's what you say when you see fireworks."

Another one burst overhead, forming into a brightly colored flower before dissipating.

"Ooh, aah," the girls said in unison and she laughed.

The girls fell asleep before the fireworks were over, but Abby was in no hurry to move. Hrebec's tail wrapped around her as she leaned against him.

"What are you thinking, my mate?" she whispered.

"I was wondering if you missed Earth."

"Why would you even think that? I have everything I need right here." She paused. "Well, there is *one* thing I need..."

"Anything."

She gave his tail a long seductive stroke, dragging her fingernails lightly across the sensitive surface. "I need some time alone with my mate."

He shuddered and his scent deepened. "I'll put the girls to bed."

Hrebec stepped into their bedroom to find that Abigail had not taken advantage of the time while he put the girls to bed to prepare for him. Instead, she was perched at the desk by the window, his father's desk, going over a series of spreadsheets on her computer screens.

"I thought you weren't going to work tonight?"

She jumped guiltily. "I wasn't going to, but Leo was so fussy today I didn't get much done."

Not long after they had first moved to the colony, she had raised a financial question at one of the community meetings that revealed the extent of her fiscal background. After that, she had been flooded with requests for assistance and it had evolved into a full-time job.

"You know you don't need to work."

"But I want to. And I think it's important that the girls see that women have choices."

"Yes, my mate," he agreed solemnly.

She laughed. "I know—I've said that a thousand times before, haven't I?"

"You may have mentioned it. As I may have

mentioned before that you are a very desirable female. I believe you said you needed me..."

The scent of her arousal perfumed the air and she closed her screens. "I do."

As she rose and walked towards him, he allowed himself to appreciate the lush curves of her body, even riper since the birth of their son. His shaft stiffened, as it did so frequently in her presence. She paused when she reached him, her fingers tracing the line of his erection through his pants.

"I find you a very desirable male," she whispered.

"Then that works out well," he said, his breath catching as she teased his sensitive head.

"I think I'm in the mood for something forbidden tonight," she said, sinking to her knees and freeing his erection.

Later that night, he heard Leo cry out on the monitor.

"He's hungry," Abigail said sleepily. "He hasn't been eating well because of the teething."

"I'll bring him to you."

He walked into the nursery to find his son pulling himself up on the crib rail and shook his head. The boy was growing so quickly. He lifted him into his arms and Leo buried his head in Hrebec's neck the same way Tiana had done at that age. His little tail circled Hrebec's arm.

When he returned to the bedroom, a soft light was glowing by the bed. Abigail was sitting up, her beautiful breasts already exposed. While Leo nursed hungrily, Hrebec watched her, admiring the sight, and more than a little tempted by the sight of her distended nipple when she moved Leo to the other side.

Outside, the rain began to fall, but the bedroom was warm and cozy in the soft lamplight. Leo's hungry suckling gradually slowed.

"He's asleep," Abigail whispered.

"I'll take him back to bed. Leave the light on. I have plans for when I return and I want to be able to see all of you."

"Mm, that sounds—"

Lightning flashed outside the window. Unlike the earlier fireworks show, this was not silent, and a crack of thunder immediately followed. His eyes met Abigail's, hers alive with laughter.

"You know what that means," she said.

Sure enough, two heads were already peeking around the door frame.

"Tiana was scared," Lucie said.

"Was not." Tiana scowled at her sister.

There was another crack of thunder and the girls leaped for the bed.

"Perhaps both of you were a little scared," he said. "Even though you're big girls."

"Maybe," Lucie agreed. "Can we sleep with you?"

Abigail's shoulders were shaking with silent laughter, but he couldn't resist the two pleading faces. His plans for Abigail's delicious body would have to wait.

"Do you want me to put Leo back in his crib?" he asked her.

"No," Lucie said. "He might get scared too."

Since Leo was sound asleep at Abigail's breast, he didn't think that likely, but if the girls were staying, Leo might as well stay too. Abigail turned off the light and eventually, everyone settled down.

Long after his family fell asleep, Hrebec stayed awake, relishing the moment. He was lying on his back, with his son on his chest and Lucie tucked under his arm. Abigail was snuggled against his other side with Tiana curled between them. Lucie shifted in her sleep and kicked his thigh and he smiled. Some things never changed.

Outside, the thunder had died down and all that was left was the sound of the rain. The clean smell drifted into the room, mingling with the scents of his family, and he was filled with a boundless contentment. He had been so sure that the only thing waiting for him was lonely years filled with regret. Instead, he had hopes for his race, and more importantly, dreams for his own future. He smiled into the dark room and closed his eyes.

Mama and the Alien Warrior

Authors' Note

Thank you so much for reading *Mama and the Alien Warrior!* We hope you enjoyed our sweet and steamy SFR. We had such an amazing time writing about Abby and Hrebec!

How did this all come about? Well, months ago Bex asked Honey for an arc of *Anna and the Alien*, and an amazing friendship was born. Seriously, it's like we were insta/fated friends! We just clicked. Now we support each other's writing and fangirl over all things SFR.

The best part about our friendship is how our interests coincided. We wanted to explore heroines at different stages of life as they navigated the perils of alien abduction. Very niche, but we both immediately loved the idea and knew that we had to collaborate on the story.

Although we wrote *Mama and the Alien Warrior* together, we did not do it alone. We want to express our undying gratitude to our beta readers, Kathryn S., Tammy S., and Janet S. Thank you, ladies, for helping us perfect Abby and Hrebec's story!

We also want to give a huge thank you to Cameron Kamenicky and Naomi Lucas, the amazing graphic designers who created our outstanding cover. For us, it was important to depict Hrebec as a fierce alien warrior tenderly holding a human child, and Cameron and Naomi delivered.

Lastly, we'd like to thank our families. The support of our spouses and children has been phenomenal. Because of them, we chose a Mother's Day theme for our alien abduction story... If our families only knew how they inspired us!

Again, thank you so much for reading our book! It would mean the world if you left an honest review at

Amazon. Reviews help other readers find books to enjoy, which helps the authors as well!

All the best,
Honey & Bex

Other Titles

Books by Bex McLynn

The Ladyships Series
Sarda
Thanemonger

Standalone
Rein: A Tidefall Novel

Books by Honey Phillips

The Alien Abduction Series
Anna and the Alien
Beth and the Barbarian
Cam and the Conqueror
Greta and the Gargoyle
Deb and the Demon
Ella and the Emperor
Faith and the Fighter

The Alien Invasion Series
Alien Selection
Alien Conquest
Alien Prisoner

Printed in Great Britain
by Amazon

44388082R00148